To Nancy!

Thank you for your support! This has been a life long dream of mine! Your support is helping to make that dream come true! :)

Tricia

Death by
Imagination

Death by Imagination

Patricia M Brothers

Copyright

The story 'Death by Imagination' is a work of fiction. The names, characters, businesses, places, events, incidents and dialogue are drawn from the author's imagination and are not to be construed as real. Any resemblance to actual events or persons, living or dead, is entirely coincidental.

Printed in the United States of America.

First Printing, 2017

ISBN-13: 978-1-942022-88-6

ISBN10: 1942022883

The Butterfly Typeface Publishing
PO BOX 56193
Little Rock Arkansas 72215

To my beautiful girls,
Torrie and Aailyah,
I thank God that He gave you to me as a gift.
You have been a true blessing in my life.
My success is driven by your love
and wanting to give you a brighter future.
If you remember nothing else in life –
know that I love you with all of my heart
and this is for you.

To my mom (Loretta)
and sisters
(Yolanda, Rena, and Crystal),
I love you guys.

beyond imaginable

Table of Contents

Foreword

As a Publisher, I've come to expect certain things from writers and I've been made aware of others. However, meeting Author Patricia M. Brothers was an unexpected jolt from what I thought I knew and what I'd come to expect.

Her manuscript grabbed my attention from the beginning and refused to let go until the very end. Prior to reading, *Death by Imagination*, mystery and suspense was not a genre I would claim to enjoy. However, enjoyment is too small of a word for what I'm now calling, the *Patricia Brothers Experience*!

Patricia has a way of weaving words in a manner that elicits a variety of emotional (and dare I say physical) stimuli that demands the reader's attention. You will be intrigued, puzzled, angered, and least of all, aroused.

I must warn you – this book is NOT for the weak of mind, but rather for those distinguished readers who prefer challenge with their entertainment.

I've read other works by this author and she is definitely not a one hit wonder. I *expect* great things from Author Patricia Brothers and I'm keenly *aware* that she will be the one to watch as she soars high in her literary journey.

Iris M. Williams

Acknowledgments

Sam – As your birthday twin it is only fair that I thank you for your friendship and give you a 'shout out' because you are the reason I began to write again.

Aleta – Thank you for being you and my 'not so silent' partner. You have invested in me so much as a friend and I now consider you my sister.

Angie J – How could I not mention you? It is because of you that I found Iris. We may not talk all the time, but when we do, you are a true inspiration.

S. Renee Hill – No words can thank you enough for the amount of support you have given me through the years.

Iris M. Williams – A business relationship turned friendship. Thank you for making me 'jump' and for being there to guide me along the way.

Prelude

"And you are sure this is going to work," asks Derrick as he holds her hand.

"As sure as I have ever been."

"No one knows who's behind all this?"

"No one has a clue."

"What about your father?"

"Considering he's *not really* my father. I'd say it's all good."

"And your mother?"

"Well, that will be a tough one, but hey I'm in it to win it."

"Do you love me?"

"Eh. Somewhat." She laughs a teasingly laugh but Derrick is unsure of how to feel.

Deep down he really loves her, but he's not sure how far she'd be willing to go. She really just may be the death of him.

Tonight's party had all the Who's Who of the business including reputable singers, actors, producers and directors. Laura Henley knew that this was no ordinary meet and greet. She knew that she would step on some toes to get what she wanted. She grew up tough, being the only girl of six siblings. Not to mention the fact that she was the youngest and her entire family was overprotective of her. She decided to have a good time anyway.

Laura

Laura is running top speed and there is panic and fear in her breath. She knows someone is out there, but she just can't see them.

"Shit!"

She is running & fumbling through her purse looking for her keys when she drops her purse.

"Fuck!"

Laura has been running in circles for the last ten minutes trying to escape her attacker. She felt someone watching her the entire evening other than her boyfriend and felt very uneasy at the party. She had been networking all night and had a few drinks. Not enough to get her drunk, but enough to have a good buzz and that is when she felt the strange vibe. Someone staring at her. Watching her every move. Laura is used to people staring. Tonight, however, had an eerie feeling.

Who wouldn't marvel looking at her? She is a tall, slender, blonde who is always dressed to kill. Tonight she is wearing a black Armani dress with a gold belt and stilettos to match. Her hair is neatly tucked in a bun with a sparkle pin to accentuate her hair color. Some models wished they could be her.

She is a recruiter. She looks for the best of the best and if they can't match her standards, then she lets them

know. She was very cruel when it came to work.
Everyone knew to take her seriously as she often
commanded. Models knew that if there was one person
to get their career off the ground it was Laura.

Ashley Edwards (her best friend) is dressed in a red silk
dress with spaghetti straps and her hair is short and
brunette. She too owes her career success to Laura.
They have been friends since high school and even went
to the same college. No one knows the many secrets that
they hold between them except for them. Their
relationship is closer than anyone knows. So much so,
that they were often lovers or shared lovers. Although
their families never found out.

She walks over to Laura from the bar to greet her.

"Oh Laura you look *so* beautiful tonight. Is this for
someone special?"

Ashley never was afraid of showing Laura the desire
and affection that she had for her. Lightly caressing the
fabric, Laura allows Ashley to swiftly nip at her breasts
with her fingertips. They laugh their girlish laugh and
Laura steps in closer into Ashley's ear.

With a hint of sexual desire, "Of course. Can't you tell? If
Michael wasn't here, I'd let you get a peek in more." She
twirls in front of Ashley teasingly and she catches
Ashley licking her lips with desire. Ashley glances an
envious glance at Michael and knows it is only a matter
of time before he gets to taste the sweet goodness that
Laura holds like a well-kept secret.

Ashley crosses her arms and mutters, "Interesting."

"Come now Ashley. Don't tell me I hear a bit of jealousy?"

"I don't understand why you haven't told him yet."

"I will in due time. He hasn't quite been "broken in" yet."

"Did you forget that last night when *we* were in bed together, you told me you slept with him?"

"Yes, I know."

"Then why doesn't he know about us?"

"Because I haven't found a way to tell him how to *share*," Laura laughs at the idea of sharing her is like a four-year-old with a toy.

"I hardly find it funny. Why tonight he gets to have you all to himself?"

"Um, you do realize that you had me to yourself practically all through college and including last night?"

"True, but I want you so bad right now. I can taste you on my lips and that dress is not helping any."

"Good then I've done my job." Laura walks away to mingle with other guests leaving Ashley to sulk in the bitter sweet idea of not being able to have her at the moment.

Ashley walks away and finds her herself attracted to another brunette who is gently rubbing her husband's arm. If she didn't know better, you would have sworn it was her looking at herself in the mirror.

Guests are making their way around laughing, eating and drinking. Each guess is dressed accordingly. The people who have been in the industry the longest were more casual than the "new money" that just stepped on board.

A waiter approaches Laura with a glass of her favorite wine and she automatically raises her glass to Michael Clay as he does the same gesture back to her.

After taking a few sips, she then slips out of present company and seductively walks up the stairs holding the glass in her right hand while gripping the railing ever so lightly with her left.

They watch from a distance. **They** see that she is not alone and waits for a more opportune time. She will be alone soon enough. Then vengeance will be for the taking.

Laura is not above reproach and she shall pay for her haughtiness. She must pay. It will justify all the years of longing and suffering. All the time waiting for the moment to make her pay.

Michael and Laura have found a room off of the east wing of the mansion. Michael is six feet two inches with a wrestler's body. His hair is dark brown with green eyes. He's definitely worth taking a second glance at. He's just Laura's type; handsome, smart and rich. Michael begins to rub his hands all over Laura as she gently unbuttons his shirt and kisses his chest. When she gets to the final button, she begins to unzip his pants and frees his throbbing member.

He moans as she gently rubs her hand across it. He lifts her up and lightly throws her across the bed. He then proceeds to pull her underwear off only to realize she is not wearing any. To which he then slides his fingers across her to feel how wet she is. She lets out a gasp as he begins to kiss and caress her thighs as he uses one hand to unbuckle her belt and then pulls off her dress.

She lifts up to allow him easier access to her body and he delights in how exquisite she looks. She slides down under him to kiss him passionately and fiercely. She reaches her first climax as he enters two fingers into her and smoothly pulsates inside of her. She groans in anticipation for the real thing. "Do it," she softly whispers as he lifts her up to enter her, there is a loud bang on the door. They both jump and laugh.

"That had to be Robert. What a jerk" she laughs as she knows that since this is Robert's party and house – it had to be him.

Michael grabs her and holds her close – softly kissing her. "Well, you know, I know of a place where we can go and there won't be *any* interruptions." He lightly kisses her shoulders. "Interested?"

Laura purrs like a kitten and rubs her head into his neck and shoulders.

"Definitely. I need it right now" she gasps as she grasps onto him like she is about to lose her mind.

"Then follow me" Michael whispers softly into her ear.

Michael and Laura quickly gets dressed and head back downstairs to mingle with the other guests.

"Babe give me a few minutes and I will go home and get things ready. Besides, I'm really not ready for everyone to know our dirty little secret."

"The only part of the secret that is dirty are the things I do for you."

"Mmm hmm just the way I like it."

"Well, we also have to talk. There is something I think you should know."

"All in due time. There is no rush baby. Tonight I just want to fuck you in that dress."

"Your wish is my command."

"Then I command that tonight we take it one step further."

"What?"

"I know about you and Ashley. I want the both of you in my bed."

Shocked, Laura puts her hand over her mouth.

"Wow! Uh how did you know?"

"It didn't take much and tonight when I saw how she interacted with you, it confirmed my suspicion. It was hot the way she slyly nipped at your breasts with her fingers. Pretending to admire your dress. I nearly came right there."

"You saw that?"

"Yes and I want to see more."

Satisfied that things were actually going her way, Laura was quite happy. She got to be with the two people whom she loved dearly at one time. This put the icing on the cake.

"Well let me talk to her and see what she says. I am quite sure she is ok with it."

"Great. See you in fifteen."

Michael leans in for a quick kiss of the cheek and walks away.

Laura walks away to find Ashley and give her the good news. She is beaming, but when she gets that feeling again – her high diminished. However, it was not about to stop the fun filled action that was sure to be a pleasure tonight.

The pure thought of being the center of attention and having Michael and Ashley catering to her every sexual need drew Laura over the edge. As she walked she could feel how wet she was and her nipples were definitely protruding out of her dress; so much so she had to cross her arms to hide it. Laura never finds Ashley so she picks up her phone to call when she is distracted. Something isn't right.

Laura heads to get her coat. Surely by now Michael is home as he lives a few blocks away. She was so hot and bothered that as of right now if he touched her, her climax could be heard all around the neighborhood. She decided to think about work instead to bring things down a bit. She starts to walk to her car when she hears footsteps. They become louder and heavier as if someone is trying to catch up with her.

Seeing a dark figure, she begins to pick up her pace. The street is not well lit and she did not want to take any chances. She was sure that whomever is behind her is following her. She sees the figure getting closure and not wanting them to know where she parked she jots down another street and planned to return to her car once she knew it was safe to do so.

Laura makes it to the car but drops the keys. It's dark and the keys are under the car. She looks back to see if anyone is approaching. She struggles to reach the keys. Crying with anxiety, she begs to be able to reach the keys in time as the figure is now quickly approaching her. How did they catch up to her so fast?

"Shit!" She grabs the keys and unlocks the door.

She never makes it.

***

It is still night time. It's dark. She cannot tell exactly where she is. Dark and ominous music is playing in the background. She sees the same figure that had been chasing her earlier that night. They are sitting there staring at her; not moving and not flinching - just sitting there. Laura tries hard to squint to see who it is, but the shadows and the minimum light is making it hard to see.

Laura is tied to a chair. She is falling in and out of focus. She is bound and gagged. They are now hovering over her. She seems out of it; in a haze. She is unsure what these effects are. Is it from the alcohol or did they drug her? What is going on? Inside of her head she is scrambling her thoughts of any threats she had received lately. Maybe someone she just met? A guy she turned down?

A long blade beams in the light. It cuts her arm and blood trickles. She winces. There is a sinister laugh. A second blow is made to the other arm. Her eyes widen as the blade cuts her face. Although she is in imminent danger, her only thought was the scar that would be left on her face. She then confirms that they want to kill her beauty and not her. She cries out in pain and begs for mercy. Her muffled cries go unanswered. Then that same thought disappears. The figure moves behind her and she feels what is about to happen next. Her eyes widen. They pull her long blonde hair hard and slit her throat and she gives one final scream and cry.

Back at the party Laura's car is still there. She is lying there beside the car. Her body is cold and lifeless. Ashley and Robert approach to enter their car. Unaware that Laura is lying on the ground. Ashley smirks in anger with the thought of Laura being in Michael's bed tonight. She then realizes that Laura would one – never walk anywhere and two – leave her car behind.

She's Not Coming Back

As Robert Mack opens the car door of a red 4 door BMW – Ashley gets this strange feeling.

"Hmmm. I could have sworn that Laura left early to get ready for her new Beau." She tries very hard to hide her anger and jealousy.

"It seems that she and Michael make a nice couple. I wonder if he g...."

He trails off as he notices Laura's foot from the side of the car.

"What? Golf?" She chuckles, "Is that all you think about?"

His face becomes more distorted. Ashley looks in wonder at Robert.

"Helloooo?? What in God's name are you gawking at??"

She gets out of the car and notices the same thing. She grabs her heart. She runs over to Laura's body. Robert joins her and attempts to find a pulse.

"She has no pulse."

"Oh my God! Laura! Laura!"

Ashley lets out a blood curdling scream for help as she looks around for help.

"Somebody call 911! Somebody help please!!"

Robert takes out his cell phone to call 911 and gives the information. Ashley grabs Laura and rocks her. Robert takes Laura out of Ashley's arms and performs CPR. Nothing is working after an agonizing five minutes, the paramedics arrive and take over. Ashley stands there in shock and disbelief at what is taking place right now. She is shaking so hard that she cannot focus on the questions the police officer is asking of her.

The paramedics get to the hospital, but as they know – she is not coming back. The doctors still attempt to revive her and are having no luck. Triage takes over and all hope is lost. Detectives are on the scene. Robert is holding Ashley. The waiting room is quite full. Michael comes rushing through the door. The doctors are standing in the hallway speaking with two police detectives.

Detective Alana Wells is a well-dressed black female in a nice pants suit with black shoes. Her hair is black and her skin is a beautiful caramel color. If no one knew she was a detective, they would have sworn she was a model. Detective Wells glances over in Ashley's direction, thanks the doctors for their time and walks over to Ashley. Ashley couldn't help but think of how incredibly beautiful she looked. And how impressed Laura would have been with her. This sends even more tears down her face. Detective Wells reaches across the table to grab a few tissues and hand them to her.

"Did you see anything unusual?" Detective Wells asks Ashley.

Her partner Jason Finley, was dressed just the opposite. He is more business casual without a care in the world. He comes across as a nice guy but could also be crass at times. This was one of those times. His golden blonde hair is neatly combed and if he would just take an extra five minutes in grooming – he would be a nice-looking guy. He comes and stands next to her with his arms folded.

Ashley shakes her head no - still in disbelief. She shudders and nearly falls to the ground when Robert instinctively catches her. She is crying uncontrollably and begins to irritate the detectives. They are trying to be sensitive however it is hard getting the answers they need through the sobbing and tears. They have been in the game for over ten years now. Nothing surprises them anymore.

Detective Wells begins to speak again, "When was the last time you saw her before this?"

Speaking through sobs, "At, at the party. She and Michael were headed up the stairs."

Wells gives her an inquisitive look. "Michael? Who is Michael?

As she ends the question, Michael is walking up to them. "I am."

Detective Wells turns her attention to him.

"Where were you two headed?"

"To one of the spare bedrooms."

"Spare bedrooms?" She sends a quizzical look and there is an uncomfortable silence.

"She is, uh, we are ... we were 'together.' You know, we were considering marriage. We were flirting with each other. And one thing lead to another. We found an empty room and started becoming intimate. However, there was a bang on the door and we were interrupted if you know what I mean."

Raising her eyebrow, "And after that?"

"We decided to leave and go to my place to finish what we had started."

"So what happened because obviously she didn't make it?" Detective Wells leans over and gestures to the entrance that leads to the hospital morgue.

"She called and stated that she was going to stay a few minutes longer and I told her I would be waiting. I left to get things ready."

"Oh, so you must have gotten home pretty fast."

"I don't live too far from the party."

"Hmph. OK. Can anyone vouch for that?"

Michael becomes irritated.

"Yeah, my cell phone." He pulls out the cell and hands it to her to show his last calls. "The call came in at 11:30."

Finley steps up to be beside Wells as if he is protecting her.

"What about your neighbors?" Finley asks knowing full well what Michael's response will be.

"Our houses are several yards apart in addition to privacy fences. You do the math."

It dawns on him as they think he may be a suspect.

"Wait, you could not possibly believe that I did this to her? I *loved* her."

Wells begins to speak, "You know what? I don't know you from a can of paint and don't know what to believe at this point. But what I do know is, I got a dead girl over here and you were the last person with contact to her. *You* do the math. You've seen how these things go."

Wells walks off.

Finley puts a hand on Michael's shoulder.

"Do her a favor will ya? Don't think about leaving town for a while. Thanks."

He taps Michael on the arm and follows behind Wells.

It is late in the afternoon. The, Medical Examiner, is in the morgue standing over Laura. Laura's body is in full view for anyone that walks in the room. He is studying her form and shape. He is perplexed as to how in the world could such a beautifully, well-groomed woman just die? There aren't any cuts scrapes, bruises, needles marks, hemorrhaging – nothing. Nothing that could indicate her cause of death.

Alex Hemphill is a well-known M.E. He is dressed in slacks and a buttoned-down shirt with a medical coat on and black shoes. Detective Wells enters the room silently, nearly startling him. He is always happy to see her as he has been wanting her for as long as he can remember. She is just as beautiful and well-groomed as the dead body lying in front of him. A very nasty and haughty thought overwhelms him for a brief second of having them both in his bed.

He imagines touching and caressing the both of them. He closes his eyes at the thought of Laura and Alana sharing intimate kisses as he strokes himself. Be that as it may, just as quickly as the thought came – it left as he also remembers that he tries to remain professional with her. Although at times it is very hard.

Over Someone Else's Dead Body

"Well, hey! If it isn't my favorite person in the whole wide world!"

"Aw, now Alex don't you start." She gives him a coy smile as much as she stays to herself; she does at times enjoy being in his company.

"Come on now. You know I have to give you trouble. The only time I see you – is, well, over someone else's dead body."

Finley shoots a curious look. Wells steps closer to the body.

"What do we got?" as she stares at the beautiful body in front of her.

"A whole lot of nothing."

"Um", she shakes her head from side to side. "I'm sorry. I don't speak that language."

"Well you better go get the *"I'm Dead"* version of Rosetta Stone because you are looking at one perfectly intact human corpse that is healthier than the proverbial horse she rode in on."

"What are you saying?"

"What I'm saying, my love, is that all organs are accounted for and in good shape. There is not one bump, scrape, burn, bruise or blemish. Prelim Tox Reports show no drugs in her system although she did have an occasional glass of wine but not over the **B**lood **A**lcohol **L**imit. So ergo no real root cause of death. Damn, look at her nails, perfect."

Finley furrows his brows, "That does not compute." He raises an eyebrow. "A perfectly healthy person doesn't just pass out and die without there being a root cause."

Alex quickly glances at Finley and moves on. "This is true and this is the exception to the rule."

Wells moves in closer while picking up a medical glove and examines Laura's hand. "What about signs of a struggle?"

"Nope. Nothing" Alex says as he wishes it was his hand that she was holding.

"Nothing at all?" Wells shoots him a glance.

"This girl is a pre-Madonna. Clean hair, nails, toes – you name it. Oh wait. There was some semen."

Finley & Wells look at each other. "Run it."

Wells is sitting at her desk at the **D**enver **P**olice **D**epartment. She is looking over her report. Police Chief Williams stops to stare at her as she looks like her father. Very pristine, well-kept and into the job.

Nabbing a Bad Guy

"Wells, what you got for me?" Police Chief Williams asks.

"I have no idea," Wells responds with an exasperated look. "Honestly, this is the case that's hard for me to crack. I have looked at the time line. I checked on the boyfriend. The Tox Reports came in with nothing. No forensic evidence. Nothing. Not a freakin' thing. No witnesses. No other interviews outside of the people that I have already talked to. No Clue. Yet, I have this dead girl on my hands and no answers for anyone."

"There's gotta be something? What about the semen?"

"Nothing. I don't have enough to pin on the boyfriend to warrant a sample."

Finley walks up with two cups of coffee. Wells' favorite. A Carmel Latte with a shot of espresso and vanilla. The aroma is so strong it fills the precinct. Wells inhales and lets out a sharp breath.

"She's been looking at this all night. Tell her to go home." Finley says as he hands Wells the coffee.

"Is that true?" Chief Williams gives her what could be described as a loving, fatherly look.

"I just don't get it." Wells throws her hands up in defeat.

With a stern voice, Chief Williams let it be known, "It's called unsolved. Pack it up and go home."

As Wells began to pack up her belongings. The mother and brothers of Laura enters the door and walks directly to them.

Mrs. Daniels is ringing her hands in worry and concern. "Good evening detectives. Do you have anything on my daughter's killer or killers?"

Wells stands up placing a hand on her shoulder and looking her in the eye. "I am so sorry. No. We have nothing at this moment."

Laura's brother Brian looks exactly like her although they are a few years apart. "How could you have nothing? I see motive written all over this."

Wells shoots him a *so you went to school for this kind of stuff* look. "Oh? How so?"

Leo who looks nothing like his other siblings as he has red hair and green eyes. "Well, what our dear mother doesn't know is that Laura was already married. She had been married for months now and just decided to plan a wedding. Then there's the matter of the insurance policy."

Mrs. Daniels looks at her sons in dismay. "Insurance policy? What insurance policy?"

Brian steps in a little closer barely a whisper as if this was some family scandal. "Yes. Michael has a half million dollar policy on her. She told us just in case..."

Finley raises his brow, "In case what?"

Leo shrugs his shoulders, "In case something happened."

Wells is completely irritated as they should have said this in the beginning. "But he said that they were (using fingers for quotations) *in love.*"

Brian gives her a sharp look. "Oh we have no doubt he loved her. But he just loved money more."

Finley pulls out several pieces of paper and rechecks them. "I checked his financials. He's pretty clean with the exception of a few late payments."

Leo gives him a *I know a lot more look.* "Yeah, but check his mom's credit and that tells a whole other story."

Wells grabs her coat and leaves. "Well now, that's something!"

Mrs. Daniels looks to the Chief, "Wh-where's she going?"

Finley smirks, "To nab her a bad guy."

Inside of his plush corporate office, T.J. White is on the phone. All around there are pictures of his family, certificates, degrees and awards on the wall and his desk. He is well dressed and over paid. He has on a Tom Ford suit.

T.J. White, the Dead Man

"Yes, this is true. No. Your return will be much higher. The competition is no match for me. Science is easy. I imagine the formulas will be sent to you overnight, considering. No problem thanks."

His secretary enters the room and he shoots her a - *I can fuck you right now glance.* Things must be going his way and she loves it when he is having a great day. She is dressed corporate with a full skirt suit on. She whispers, "Hey T.J. do you have those mark ups?"

He covers the phone and nods toward the filing cabinet. "Yes check the files." He then returns to the call. "Like I said, I think you will be very pleased with the results. No not at all. I'm sure we will be talking soon. OK. Thanks. Bye."

She glances back to confirm she has what she needs.

***

Time has passed, T.J. is still in his office looking over some work. Pretty much everyone is gone except the cleaning people and **they** are watching.

"OK, so what can I get now? Evan owes me a favor. Let's see if the bastard comes through." He picks up the phone and takes a long sip of his coffee.

He blacks out.

Evidence

Wells arrives back to the scene of Laura's death. Police are searching for more evidence. There is none.

Disgusted and visibly upset - "I don't believe this. Unbelievable." Wells places her hands on her hips.

"How can there be a crime scene with no evidence what-so-ever?" Finley stands behind her as her personal body guard.

"There is evidence we just have to find it."

"OK, yeah, um, let me know how that works out for you." He pats Wells on the back and walks away.

T.J. is now bound and gagged. He is groggy but he sees the gun on the table. His eyes widen. He looks up and sees this figure sitting next to the gun. He tilts his head as he recognizes the figure. **They** *begin to play Russian roulette. It spins and lands on the stranger. Click.* **They** *do not flinch. It spins and lands on T.J.. Click. T.J. jumps in horror and lets out a sigh of relief. It spins again and lands on T.J.. T.J. through muffled cries, begins to plead with the stranger. Click. He jumps. It spins again and lands on T.J.. T.J. is counting the rounds and mentally is trying to figure out his odds. Click. It spins again and it lands on T.J.. Click. By now T.J. figures that this is some kind of prank and totally relaxes. It spins and lands on T.J.. Bang. Blood splatters all over the wall and floor.*

The Next Day

It is the next day and T.J. is back at work. He is slumped over the desk. From the outside looking in, it looks as if he had been at work all night and fell asleep.

Alice his secretary walks over to the filing cabinet and replaces the file.

"OK, I think if you are going to sleep at work the least you could do is lie on the couch in the break room. Or is that too much like therapy?"

There is no response from T.J.. He is just lying there.

Alice glances over his way, "What no sexual innuendo today?" She laughs and walks over to T.J.. She shakes his shoulder. "T.J.? T.J.?!" Her eyes are in horror as she feels his cold, dead and limp body. She lets out a scream that can be heard from down the hall. David runs in and sees T.J..

"Oh my God. Call 911!" David yells over his shoulder.

David grabs Alice and backs out of the room. Alice is trembling horribly and looks at the ring that T.J. just gave her. He called her his second wife. The best wife a man could ever have. Even though she knew that he loved his *real wife* and would never leave her it still felt good to hear him say it. The night that he told her and gave her the ring, they had just made love. It was rigorous and very steamy. She had yet to tell him that she was pregnant hoping that would be enough to leave his wife.

It takes no time for the EMS, police and fire department to arrive.

As Wells and Finley are leaving the scene of Laura's death. She hears the call over the radio. She doesn't hesitate to put on the sirens and head over to where T.J.'s body is still at his desk. Alana lives her life on the radio and made it almost simultaneously.

Wells enters the room and is disgusted to see how the other officers are not following protocol. "What do we got?"

The First Response Officer intimidated by Wells speaks, "Honestly, none of us know."

"How do you *not* know?" She says irritated.

Finley steps up and in between Wells and the officer. Wells' hands are balled up in a fist and the look on her face is not a good one.

"OK. Let's see what evidence you *do* have."

The First Response Officer responds hesitantly, "Nothing."

Wells frowns so hard that her face looks like a pit-bull.

"Again, with the nothing!" as she throws up her hands in disgust.

"The only thing we could find was a cup of coffee."

"It's called evidence. Bag it. And have any and all results sent to me directly."

"Yes ma'am." The First Response Office leaves in a hurry.

Finley walks over to the body and begins to do a general examination.

"No injuries or wounds and the body's been here a while. Spoke with some of the people and they all said he was working late. Only people here were cleaning."

Wells turns a raised eyebrow to him.

"And??"

"Everyone checks in and out every time they walk through the doors and no one seemed suspicious."

"Seemed? Video?"

"Malfunctioning."

Wells lets out an exasperated sigh.

"Figures. Get him over to the M.E." (Finley snickers)

"Watch it."

Detective Wells enters the room with a look of I'm tired of this bullshit on her face. At the same time Alex has another sexual fantasy of the dead man, him and Alana in a room together. For some reason Alex really wants Alana right now. Maybe because she has taken off her jacket and he has a great view of her supple breasts. The sun is beginning to set.

Nothing Significant

"Look, I have a lot to cover and the media is already talking," Detective Wells announces.

"Um, well, see what had happened was...," Alex throws up his hands and chuckles.

"Noooooo ," Detective Wells says. "I don't want to hear it." Covering her ears with her hands and lets out a laugh. It struck Alex as weird as he never really heard her laugh before like this, but he loves it. She continues. "And who have *you* been around?"

"I saw it on T.V." Alex says and the two laugh.

"Please give me something," Alana pleads.

"I did." He smirks as he slyly undresses her with his eyes.

Alana whispers and moves in closer (maybe she likes him a little) – "Your phone number doesn't count."

"Man." (Exhales.) "OK. He consumed a great deal of coffee. He was however – how do you say – a weed head. But, outside of that – so far - nothing significant. Tox Prelim only showed he likes marijuana and a whole lot of it."

"Ugh!" Alana sighs in frustration.

"Wells. There is something weird going on."

"I know. I will be back. Please get me some data or evidence somehow. I need to get a handle on this as soon as possible."

"I will see what I can do Wells, but there are no guarantees."

"Thanks." She walks away and Alex just stares at her. He never noticed how supple her ass was until now and all he wants to do is fuck it. He imagines that she is just as freaky as he is and he hopes one day to find out.

***

Alana is home preparing a glass of wine and looking over the reports. She sighs. "How can two perfectly healthy people – sort of – just drop dead and die? What am I missing?" (**They** are watching her.)

She sits for hours. Pouring glass after glass. She finally sets everything down, stretches and gets up to walk around. She turns on the t.v to see a news reporter standing outside of T.J. White's office building:

This is the second unexplained death in a matter of weeks and the police have no clue. So far the police have been ineffective in their investigation. Recent reports blame Police Chief Williams for hiring incompetent staff. City leaders are calling for officers to be retrained. Rumors are flying on how the police fumbled over the deceased's body and evidence. It seems unlikely that a conviction would occur even if there was a suspect.

Wells cocks her head to the side, turns off the television and goes to bed.

There are children playing in the park. Mothers are gathered together. This is no ordinary park. This park is more like an amusement park. There are several types of slides, rides, trails, tennis courts, and pavilions for parties, there is an indoor and outdoor pool and a large man-made lake. This park is unbelievably large and sits in the middle of suburbia and every family enjoys it.

Lisa Myles is sitting with a group of mom friends watching the kids playing. Each mom is in an ideal position; able to watch the play group from afar, but close enough to be there for an "oowwee".

The ladies are dressed age appropriately and quite comfortably. It's the park and usually they all take a few laps on the track to stay in shape. Today they decided to "sit and sip".

At the Park

"OK this whole thing is starting to creep me out," Lisa says. "The news says that there's a killer in the area? Jazz what do you think?"

Jazmine aka Jazz is the actual "cool mom". She stays relaxed in any situation. Once her daughter broke her arm in 3 pieces and the bone was protruding out and with blood spewing everywhere. She just grabbed a large towel wrapped her arm and left for the ER. While her husband stood there calling 911. All the while she's talking to her daughter (who is screaming at the top of her lungs) as if they are going on a shopping trip.

"Lisa girl, look you can't believe everything in the news. It's like they just want you to know to be careful. It was one woman and one man. They don't know of any links to either one. So, don't go freaking out." Jazz said as reassuring as she could.

The other moms nod in approval. Jazz is the female alpha. She has been around the block so to speak. Before Jazz, the moms had no real purpose or conversation topics. When Jazz moved in she was automatically stereotyped and many people avoided her. Now they flock to her for advice and friendship.

"But, they died with no cause." Lisa said.

"'No cause' that they are willing to disclose at this time. You never let your left hand know what the right hand is doing." Jazz responded.

"But both were well off. Like many of us." Lisa insisted.

"And? What is your point? So you think that they killing people cause they got money now?" Jazz laughs at her naiveté.

The other women shift a little uncomfortably.

"Well...," Lisa pauses. She turns as she feels something is wrong. "Michael," she yells to her son. "Stay close honey."

"You can tell you are a first-time mom." Jazz laughs and the other ladies agree.

Lisa continues to shift uncomfortably and begins to have a panic attack. She glances back and realizes that whom she thought was Michael is not. She turns left and right. She stands up. She doesn't see Michael. She walks away from the group heading towards the slide where she last saw him.

The other ladies join in the search. Finally, they agree to call the police.

"Girl, they gonna find him and he's gonna be ok.," Jazz says confidently. "Did we even call home to see if he walked home? Come on. We gotta keep looking and call your husband."

Everyone in the park is searching for Michael. There are no signs of him. Lisa calls out asking if he is playing a game to come out now. She slumps near a tree realizing that she hasn't even called her husband. The idea of never seeing her little boy is taking a serious toll on her and they have only been searching for a few hours. Jazz sits next to her near tears herself and rubs her shoulder.

They Have Michael

Michael is sitting in a chair eating ice cream in the same room as the others. Cartoons are playing in the background. There are plenty of toys strewn about the floor as if they had been recently played with. Michael is devouring the ice cream as he says "Mommy never lets me have this much ice cream before dinner."

"So, is the ice cream good Michael?"

Michael greedily and with a grunt replies, "Um hmm."

"Is it your favorite?" **They** ask.

"Um Hmm."

"Yes – chocolate is my favorite too."

They ruffle Michael's hair and Michael rubs his eyes as if he is sleepy. He quietly pushes the bowl out of the way and lays his head down. The shadowy figure picks him up and carries him off.

Lisa's house is a quaint family home. There are family pictures on the walls. It has basic but extravagant furniture throughout the home. Although there are children in the home – everything has its place. The toys are neatly put away in the baskets and there is not a speck of dust to be found. There is a basket for shoes as you enter the door, but today no one is concerned about that.

Michael is home lying in his own bed. Lisa walks in and goes up stairs crying – sobbing. She heads to her room and she is dreading walking past his room. His door is cracked open just enough to peek in. She catches something out of the corner of her eye, opens the door and rushes in to find his lifeless body. She really breaks down. Jazz runs upstairs to see what is the matter.

Not Like This

The police know this scene all too well. They give her a moment before heading up the stairs. Calvin Myles, Michael's father stands in shock not knowing really what to do. Alana slowly begins to ascend the stairs. She stops to turn to see who is behind her. News travels fast and Alex was not too far away.

"OK it is really something when they get you out. Alex what are you doing here?" Alana asks.

"I had to see it for myself. I don't believe it. As much as I want to – these are the ones that are hard to stomach." Alex reports.

"What? Homicide is every day." Alana says.

"Not like this, Wells. Not like this." Alex nods his head towards the stairs. The First Responding Officer escorts her to the room.

They go up the stairs to Michael's room. Lisa is still holding him and refusing to let go. The paramedics are trying to convince her to give them her son to place on the gurney. Jazz is standing in the corner crying uncontrollably and in disbelief. She would never had guessed in a million years that it would be this close to home. She never would have guessed that someone would do this to a baby. She just wants to be home now holding her babies tight. With everyone in the room the escape is difficult at the moment.

"Ma'am," Alana says and gently wraps her arms around Lisa. "You have to let go. I mean. We need to take your son so that we can perform an exam and see what happened. Would you allow my friends here to take Michael? I promise they will be gentle. They will take very good care of him. I promise."

Lisa sobs, "No. I let him go once and look at what happened."

"I am so sorry but you have to let us do our job if you want us to find out what happened and who did this," Alana says. "This is Alex. He's really great. He will take good care of your baby, but you have to let him do his job. I promise you this; I *will* find whoever did this and they *will never* see the light of day again. I have to ask you some questions though. OK?" She rubs Lisa's arm in comfort.

"OK." Lisa agrees and she lets go of her son.

As the EMS prepare to take Michael's body to the morgue, Lisa faints.

It is midafternoon and the police station is deathly silent. No screaming. No yelling. No arrest. For this one moment in time all is quiet. There is no police chatter. No radio chatter. Nothing. It is very eerie. Someone coughs in the distance, but no one moves. No one gives it any thought. The death of Michael softened even the burliest of men.

The Police Station

Wells is at her desk. In walks Finley with the usual Joe only larger.

Wells and the Chief are speaking.

"OK 3 dead bodies. No real link to the victims except for the "area" in which they live or work. No evidence. Not one finger print. Not one hair. Not one foot print. Either you guys are slacking or this person is superior. And I know you, (looks at Wells) - so how is it that this person can get past you?"

"I don't know Chief. I have looked and searched. The M.E. and Forensics. This is crazy! I have tried different angles and I have found none. This is a baby this time. Who would do this to a baby?"

Finley lifts an eyebrow, "Someone with a really high grudge against the parents?"

Wells just stares at Finley.

Mr. Lingerman is the fatherly type. He cares for every single person that works for him. He is in the best pristine shape of his life for his age. A very good-looking gentleman. He built the company from the ground up singlehandedly. Everyone looked up to him. Even though he is the caring type, he can also be just as ruthless and cutthroat.

Lingerman Technologies *(before T.J. dies)*

In the lab of Lingerman Technologies – Board Room Meeting.

"OK people, the Department of Defense is looking for some new toys. Any ideas?"

T.J. White had always been Mr. Lingerman's right-hand man and second in command since his intern days.

"Oh!" T.J snaps his finger. "The Chemical Team and I have come up with a few ideas."

"Bioweapons," Mr. Lingerman asks. "Care to share?"

T.J. laughs confidently. "Not in public."

"OK come to my office after lunch."

"Will do." T.J. Smirks.

It is early in the morning. In the house of Wells no one sleeps in. A few years before Alana became a detective. She's in college. Her brother is sitting next to her eating breakfast. They are two years apart. Their mother, Cynthia Wells is standing at the stove with a cup of coffee. In walks their father, Adam Wells Sr. in uniform.

The Younger Years

Adam Wells walks into the kitchen and kisses his Alana on the forehead and punches Derrick Wells, Alana's brother in the arm.

He turns to his wife. "I could have sworn that when kids go off to college they're not supposed to come back." (He Laughs) "How's my favorite Brainiac and officer-to-be?"

Together they respond dryly. "Hi Dad."

"You know the routine," Adam says. "What have you learned new?" He looks directly at Derrick.

"I'm in chemical mixes." Derrick reported

"And?" Mr. Wells continued.

This was not the ordinary "and". This "and" had a meaning. From what Derrick gathered, he felt that his father was uninterested. But still he continues.

"What I hope to discover is, putting together something that will save lives." He says proudly.

"Hopefully, beyond the cure cancer thing and AIDS I hope." Adam responds carelessly.

"Um, yeah, stuff that would help the Department of Defense," Derrick says excitedly. "You know. Homeland Security stuff."

Now Adam's interest perks up. "OK. Spill."

"Well I can't say much more," Derrick says cautiously. "What I can tell you is that I have a job lined up with Lingerman Technologies right after I graduate."

"Six Figures?" Adam pushes.

"No five, but if you round it off to the nearest. Then you can say six." Derrick laughs.

"Uh huh. Well. OK," Adam dismisses the conversation and turns to his daughter. "And you?"

Alana is clearly the apple of her father's eye. He always had a soft spot in his heart for her. Even when he is being stern with her.

"Ugh. I was hoping you would be *so* fascinated with him that you would forget about me!" Alana says.

"Fascinated? Yes. Forget about you? No. How could I forget the one that followed in my footsteps?" Adam confesses.

Derrick looks on in disgust.

"Well. Let's see," Alana thinks. "I learned how to process a crime scene."

"Live one?" Her father asks.

"Um, God no. Classroom exercise. We go live next month though. I shake every time I think about it." Alana admits.

"You will do fine." Adam says confidently.

"I know they *both* will," Mrs. Wells interrupts. "They take after their Mom."

Alana bellows out the heartiest of laughs.

Alana pulls up to Derrick's house. It is rustic. She sits in the driveway a minute deciding whether or not she wants to go in. She hasn't spoken to her brother since everything began. She walks up to the door and as she begins to knock, Derrick opens the door. It startles her a bit. She steps inside and glances around. Derrick & Alana are in the living room talking when he pours her a glass of wine.

More Than She Can Imagine

"So, detective. How's business?"

She shrugs her shoulders. "Business is business. Although, I wouldn't classify this as business."

"I understand. Talk to Dad lately?"

"Of course not! I have 3 murder cases with no known connection. One happens to be a child and no suspects? Are you trying to get me disowned?"

Derrick Snickers. "Come now Lil Sis, why on earth would I do that? I am going to tell though." (Really laughs.)

She gives a loud gasp with a stern look.

"You wouldn't?"

"Of course I would. Little Miss Perfect just can't figure it out!" (Teasingly) "Ha. Ha. Ha. Ha. Ha. When Daddy finds out!"

"You know that Dad is omnipresent & omniscient. He knows any way. So nah." She sticks out her tongue like she used to do when they were little.

They both laugh – agreeing that it is true.

"That's why we couldn't get into trouble. He literally has eyes and ears all over the place. Even today."

"I know! Imagine me even more since I work the same force he did."

Derrick nods in agreement, but he is very eager to change the subject.

"New man?"

"Nope. No time."

"Just don't want to."

"That too." She gets up and kisses him on the forehead. "Well *Bug* Brother. I gotta go. Lotta work tomorrow."

She laughs internally as she remembers how fascinated Derrick was with bugs when they were growing up. So instead of calling him *Big Brother* she calls him *Bug Brother.*

"Oh wait. I have to give you something." He exits quickly towards the kitchen.

She glances around the room and looks at some papers and files lying around. She picks them up. Her facial impressions say that she is impressed by what she sees. Derrick returns with a cake lit with candles and a present.

"Happy Birthday baby girl. I bet you thought I forgot." He smiles.

"Oh my God. What did you do?" She forgot that it was her own birthday.

"Only for my baby girl. I made it special for you. It's your favorite. Sit, you have to blow out the candles and make a wish."

She leans over to blow out the candles. Her wish is even more than she can imagine.

The sun is just barely peeking over the clouds. The entire ride Alana drives in silence thinking about everything in her life up to this moment. She would have sworn she was about to go into a midlife crisis and she is nowhere near her 50's let alone 40's. She contemplates a career change, however she knows she is good at what she does. One day though, something has to give.

She thinks long and hard about giving Alex a chance. Considering she saw how long and hard he was when she walked in the room and took off her jacket. She saw the exact moment he looked at her breasts even though he was pretty good about playing it off. She is a detective so nothing goes unnoticed around her. Like she caught Finley staring at her while she changed shirts. He probably thought she didn't know, but she gave him a pass. She walks through the door clearing her throat to keep him from having a heart attack.

Blowing Off Steam

"So, tell me what you know about Darmstadtium?"

"Hi Alex. How are you? Why I'm fine Detective Wells. Thank you for asking. And yourself? Well. You know. Same old stuff. Just a different day."

"I'm so sorry," Alana says. "I have a lot on my mind."

"I understand. Well, honestly I never heard of it. Let alone try to pronounce it. Where'd you see that?" Alex asks.

"Nowhere," Alana says wishing to change the subject.

"So Wells. Why is it that you won't give me a chance?"

"Never mix business with pleasure." She says quickly.

"Or are you just scared of pleasure?" Alex teases.

"Uh. Uh. Can you give me something? I need answers." Alana asked changing the subject yet again.

"Nope. I couldn't even if I wanted to. I've gone over everything with a fine tooth comb. Nada. Sorry." Alex said.

"OK. I just don't get it. After baby boy, everything just seems – off."

"You aren't the only one feeling this way Alana. If you need me, I'm here for you. Seriously. No innuendos intended."

"Thank you," Alana responds. "Let's get a room."

Alex drops the tools that he had in his hand. "Really?"

"Yeah. I need to blow off some steam."

"I thought you'd never ask. Let me clean up," He glances over at the two corpses lying on the table. "They aren't going anywhere."

Alana and Alex pull up to the Ritz. Alex looks more nervous than Alana. He tries to relax, but this has been a long time coming. He walks in and books the room. After paying, he goes into the gift shop and purchases a few items. He arranges for hotel room service to bring a meal and champagne. He walks to the elevator and texts her the room number as he gets into the elevator. He leaves the door propped open.

He quickly disrobes and jumps in the shower. It is heavenly. As he enjoys the shower, he doesn't notice Alana is watching him. She then too disrobes and slides in the shower with him. She begins caressing his shoulders. He melts. The tension that was once there, slowly fades away. He leans in to kiss her and she is ready for it. He grabs her hair and pulls her head back. He slides his tongue up from her neck to her chin to her lips. The anticipation is killing her.

He licks her lips and she is begging for more. However, she says nothing not really wanting to give in that quickly. He senses she is holding back so he takes charge. He slams her against the shower wall groping her and kissing her. She involuntarily moans in excitement as she was not expecting it. She had to admit to herself that he is really impressing her at this moment.

He lifts her up and bites into her neck. She loses all control. He lifts her higher and licks her nipples. She is praying that he goes even further and as she rises further into the air she climaxes and he never flinches. He lets her down slowly allowing her to gain her composure. They finish their shower and head for the bed. He lifts her up and gently places her on the bed.

For this moment in time – she forgets everything. She melts at his every touch. It feels so good. She can't imagine the last time she felt this good. For now she will just enjoy it, however she will not let her emotions get in the way. There is no way she can have a relationship with someone she works so closely with. A part of her regrets getting involved, but the sexual deviant side of her is greedily savoring every moment.

Out of Place

While Alana is back at the hotel having the lustful moment of her life; Derrick is home looking at the papers and notices that they are out of place. He tries to recollect his thoughts. Did someone come in the house? He looks around and nothing seems to be missing or moved. Just the papers. Did T.J.'s goons break in? What was his real connection to all of this? Who else knew what was going on? Now that he's dead, who is the next target? He goes over to the door. No sign of forced entry. There are barely any scratches on the doorknob. The only other person would be Alana, but she would have no real interest in this. The only thing he can think of is maybe he brushed passed them and just can't really recall. He brushes the whole thing off and heads out the door.

Derrick is at Lingerman Technologies. Derrick is with the chemical team. His face is showing some concern. They are having a brief team meeting - nothing formal. He is telling them the latest numbers and what his plans are. They all nod in agreement. They are so engrossed that they do not see Mr. Lingerman walk in. He stands back for a moment taking in how much Derrick is a phenomenal leader and team player. He clears his throat and Derrick breaks the meeting.

Derrick at Work

"Mr. Lingerman, glad to see you."

"You know Derrick. You are like a son to me. I appreciate all that you do here. How are the projects coming along?"

"Pretty good *Dad*." He jokingly laughs and winks his eye. They step away from the group.

"How are you holding up too? I know T.J. was your friend." T.J. and Derrick had been friends for years. T.J. truly was about the only friend Derrick would consider a real friend. Until T.J. started to change.

"Oh, um, fine I suppose. It's just awful."

"You know what though – I wonder if he was exposed when he was following you around."

"No sir. The prototypes are not even up and running yet. Besides, we take every precaution here."

"I know. I know. It's still a damn shame."

"I know."

"Listen. I need you to head up and finish the projects that he was working on. Business has to go on."

"Yes sir. I can. Do you mind if I pull in a few people?" Derrick asked.

"Not at all. Whatever you need. I think he was pulling some underhanded stuff anyway. I fired his secretary today. I just found out that they were having an affair. She has kept quiet all this time, but now she is having a fit because she learned she is not get any of the insurance money. She feels entitled because she is pregnant by him. It's just God awful. I do not need that kind of scandal here. Not now. She should have known better."

"Whoa. Really? You fired her?"

"Hell yes. That is not acceptable by any means. Hell, I'm willing to say he got what he deserved. You do not do that. If you are not happy leave your wife first. Besides you know that is strictly against company policy."

"True. Wow. There's way too much going on there."

"Besides. I believe the little scoundrel left her something and she is not telling. I think she is being greedy and doesn't like the fact that his wife is getting all the attention. There were plenty of rumors that he was selling information and she helped him."

"Oh man. You know everything."

"Let's just say men gossip just as much as women." Lingerman admitted.

"Well you don't have to worry about that with me," Derrick offered. "I'm pretty straight forward."

"I will admit that I am disappointed in his actions and behaviors. I really liked him and he was really going places. Damn it! Jesus. Why?"

"Well karma does not have a deadline."

"You got that right. Anyway, let me get out of your way. I just had to come and check on you."

"Thank you sir. By the way, if you would have said that in front of my Grandma – she would have given you such a tongue whippin'."

Mr. Lingerman looks puzzled then chuckles. "Yeah, well. Good thing she's not around then."

He walks off patting Derrick on the back. Derrick looks on. He really wished that the man in front of him really *was* his father. At least Mr. Lingerman had faith in him.

Alana and Finley are sitting at her desk. Finley is sitting on the corner with one leg propped up. Finley, at this point is without a care about what is going on with these murders. His only concern is for Alana. She seems over the edge and relaxed at the same time. Something happened. He just can't put his finger on it. He knows that she gets into her work. Today she just looks different. If he didn't know better he would think that she finally got laid.

I Want To Quit

Wells is looking at the files. She swears under her breath. "You know what, if I get one more body – I am leaving the country." She throws the files on her desk.

"There you go again talkin' 'bout leavin'." Finley teased.

"Do you understand who MY FATHER is? I swear if he could he would be here right now taking over my investigation."

"Well that just may be a reality." He nods toward door.

"No way," Alana gasped as she watched her father walking towards her. "Um! Hi Dad! What are you doing here?"

"As if you have to ask?" Adam says.

"Told you," Finley whispers to Alana.

"You know Chief Williams and I are really good friends. He asked if I could come over and lend a hand."

"You weren't kidding." Finley whispers again to Alana.

Alana shakes her head no.

"OK hand me everything," Adam says to Alana. "Where is the Chief?"

"In the office," Alana says and looks over her shoulder. "Dad..."

She trails off as Adam looks in disbelief. He throws a hand up at her as if he doesn't want to hear her excuses.

Finley notices Wells' eyes are tearing up.

"Let's get out of here and get some air until he's up to speed." He suggests.

They leave and her father does not acknowledge that she has left. He just takes her chair and pulls up to her desk as if he owns it. She scoffs. Finley grabs her arm and pulls her out the door. He knows that her blood is boiling and what happens next may end up with her behind bars.

As they walk to their car, Alana fumes, "You should have let me punch him."

"Number one. That is your father. Number two. He would NOT hesitate to prosecute you," Finley cautions her. "So, let's not. You need a break and a 3rd pair of eyes can't hurt."

"Ugh! It just burns me," Alana says heatedly. "He's gonna take over, solve the case and then he gets the credit. Hell! He would get the credit any way because I am his daughter. I can hear it now. 'Detective Adam Wells has much to be proud of. His daughter, Alana has cracked the case of the century. She took after his footsteps and it shows. Blah. Blah. Blah.'"

Finley chuckles because he knows she is telling the truth.

"Well. Let me buy you lunch. Food always makes you feel better. I think you are hangry."

"Boy, don't you know. Let's go to Murphy's."

Does Anyone Ever Go Home

Derrick is alone. He is working on experiments. He smiles as he knows he has accomplished something big.

"Well son," Mr. Lingerman says as he walks into Derrick's office. "Judging by the look on your face, I think I am going to be proud of you once again."

"This is true. This is true." Derrick confirms. The two men shake hands.

"Well, come join me in my office for a cup of coffee and let's discuss it." Lingerman says.

"Coffee," Derrick asks with a raised eyebrow. "Sure."

"You know I love my *special* blend." Mr. Lingerman laughs sarcastically.

"Yes. You have such exquisite taste sir."

"With all that has been going, I think it's well deserved."

"Truer words have never been spoken."

"You work so hard Derrick," Lingerman acknowledged. "Do you ever go home?"

"No sir. It doesn't feel like it. Plus no one to go home to."

"A good looking guy like you? I find that hard to believe."

"Yeah, well. It's true. Besides. I want to be sure that I am stable before I get into anything serious."

"Very good son. That makes perfect sense. Don't mess up when you do get into one either. That was T.J.'s downfall."

"I won't let you down sir."

"I know you won't. Now. How about that coffee?"

"Absolutely."

After a few hours, the two part ways. Mr. Lingerman decides to head back to his office and review T.J.'s files. He is looking for discrepancies. He wants to stay on top of things in order to avoid scandal.

They have his wife. There is a tank. Mrs. Lingerman is tied to a chair. The tank is quickly filling up. She is panicking the water is waist high and rising. The water continues to rise – slowly. **They** stand facing her outside the tank. With both hands on the tank **they** relish in her agony watching her panic and pant heavily. She is muffled. Her muffled cries going unanswered.

The water continues to rise. She sits there. She has given up knowing she is going to die. She leans her head back as if she is relaxing. Her breathing is slowing. The water is now up to her neck. She looks over to them one more time and closes her eyes. The water is now above her head and she begins to spasm until she finally stops moving.

Time to Make Money

Derrick is in the lab with the team. There is much commotion as today is an exciting day. The Department Of Defense is there to shop ideas and Derrick is feeling very confident.

"OK ladies and gentleman today is show and tell. Let's go and impress the D.O.D."

Tech 1: "Better yet – let's go make a few million dollars."

Tech 2: "I hear that! Now you're talkin'."

Tech 1: "Talkin' the talk AND walkin' the walk. Grab those folders we will need those in the meeting."

"I already have everything else in the conference room. So let's go impress the man!"

Tech 1: "Which one? The oppressor?"

"The man is always the oppressor." Everyone laughs.

Everyone is walking and talking heading to the Conference Room. It is a lavish conference room with high back chairs. There is cherry oak furniture and a large projector. Mr. Lingerman is smiling with approval. Derrick feels even more confident as he walks in the room. In Derrick's mind – Mr. Lingerman was his real dad. Hands down if he wanted to make anyone proud it was Mr. Lingerman.

The project meeting goes without a hitch. Everyone is excited as they have closed the deal of the century. The things that they will do next. Derrick is most excited as he just received an on the spot promotion. The only thing he can think about is calling his sister to celebrate. Speaking of. Where is she? He wonders. He makes a mental note to call her to see how she's been holding up.

Fight or Flight

It is a very bright and sunny morning. However, Alana is not feeling so bright or sunny. The sun beams into the police station as if the heavens opened up just for her. Again, there is nothing for her to be cheerful for. She wants to just get out of here. Hopefully. If she has her way, that will be soon enough.

She is on the phone speaking with the airlines when Finley walks in.

"Yes please. A one-way ticket to Cape Verde. The earliest flight available. Thanks yes please hurry and call me back."

Finley gives her a quizzical look. "And what in God's name are you doing?"

"I *so* cannot do it anymore. Last night, my *father* ripped me a new one."

"I thought he chewed it 'cause it does look a little flat." He takes a small peek in the back and laughs.

"Not funny. I CRIED! I literally sat there and cried like I was 15 again. Unbelievable!" Alana said with defeat. "And to make matters worse, YOU have another homicide and guess what? NO EVIDENCE!"

"What did your dad say?" Finley asked with surprise.

"WE (pointing to herself and Finley) missed something," Alana said with sarcasm. "So I'm letting him do this one."

"OK Stop. Now you are going too far. What happens when he discovers what no one has – do you really want that?" Finley asked.

"No!"

"OK so think the impossible."

"Like what." Alana said at her wits end.

"Totally outside of the box."

"How far stretched can you go? It still has to make sense." Alana said.

"Sometimes the things that don't make sense do. Like it don't make sense for you to run out of the country. But it does because you are afraid of disappointing your father." Finley explained.

"You know what? Thanks."

"No seriously. You have to think extreme. It's your only option right now."

"Extreme would be farfetched."

"So how *farfetched* can you go?"

"Who knows? For all I know this could be an inside job. I wouldn't put it past anyone at this point. Maybe I should re-interview some people."

"That's a start. But how much has your father done?"

"I don't know. He must have something he either doesn't want to tell me or he thinks I'm too incompetent to comprehend," Alana sighed. "Either way – he's not saying a word."

"So look through the file." Finley advised.

"Can't it's locked up tight."

"Wow. He takes the job a little too serious eh?"

"You have absolutely no idea. When I used to play detective when I was little, he would tell me all the things I did wrong. From processing the crime scene to looking around the body. I wanted to vomit."

"Oh man. That's right. I remember now."

"Yeah."

The phone rings. Alana picks it up. It is the airline returning her call.

"Yeah? OK! Thank you! On second thought - hold that ticket. I may not be taking that flight right now. Thank you."

Finley looks at his watch. "Time to see your boyfriend."

"Let's go." Alana blushed.

"Did I say something?"

"No."

"Then why did your face and attitude change?" Finley questioned.

"Because you are reading into it too much."

"Are you sure because from this angle – it sure looked like it."

"Then you need to change your angle and let's go. I don't have time for the Mickey Mouse Reindeer Games."

Time to See Alex

Alex is pouring over a body. It's Mrs. Lingerman. Another well preserved body. There is nothing missing or out of place. Her hair is damp. She is still wearing her jewelry and clothes from the previous night. Wells and Finley stand and watch him for a few minutes. Deep down Alana wants nothing more than for him to dominate her like he did before. They finally walk in and interrupt his train of thought.

"Alex I need some help here. Now we're talking four murders. You gotta give me something." Alana pleads.

"I can't give you what I don't have."

"What about the autopsies?"

"Didn't need to do any since everything checked out."

"What do you mean?" Alana asked.

"No missing organs. These people were not sick. Nothing."

"It's still homicide and suspicious. I thought this was protocol."

"But there's no proof."

"BUT I have dead bodies. Doesn't that warrant anything?"

"No, especially if the family objects to it." Alex reasons.

"But you could be missing something," Alana says. "Look my Dad's all over this and I just can't…"

"I know."

"We're exhuming the bodies."

"Do you know what that's going to take?"

"Yep and I'm going for it."

(Their voices become elevated and Finley feels like the odd man out.)

"You can't go against family wishes." Finley says.

"You wanna bet," Alana challenges. "I gotta get something and this will be what I need."

"Autopsying the bodies won't solve anything. You have tox reports and everything else. That's not going to happen Alana," Alex objects. "You can't go against the family. No cuts. No bruising. Nothing. I know how much you want to close this, but pulling those bodies out of the ground isn't it!"

"You aren't giving me anything. I need something."

"There is nothing. You have no evidence that this is really even a homicide. They are treating it this way because it is unsolved. You never know. It could be something toxic. It could be in the water, the food whatever."

"Exactly. And you haven't come up with ANYTHING. Aren't you supposed to be the expert? At this point it doesn't hurt to try."

"I can't fight you on this." Alex concedes.

"I know you can't. So don't even try. If you even remotely try and stop this ... So help me God! I will..." She stops short as Finley rolls his eyes at her. "Whatever." Pointing her finger with a serious attitude "You already know."

She walks off leaving both Finley and Alex perplexed. Both are staring in disbelief as she walks out the door. She hits the door so hard that the small window cracks.

Reflection: Derrick

Derrick is home thinking over his day and organizing some papers. He comes across an old photo of him and Lisa. A mix of emotions fill him quickly. Anger, hurt, jealousy, happiness and now concern. He closes his eyes and reflects on the day that he left her and wonders would things have been different.

It is late in the afternoon. Lisa and Derrick are walking down the hall towards the door to leave. Derrick looks very happy and carefree. Lisa stops short. The look on her face has him worried that something is wrong. He turns to face her and grabs her hand. She pulls back and he looks at her with apprehension.

"Hey babe. What's wrong?" Derrick asked.

"You know Derrick, I have a lot on my mind. We need to talk later." Lisa said.

"Why not now?"

"Just later ok?"

"No. You know I don't move like that. Say it now and just get it over with. If something is wrong, we can fix it." Derrick insisted.

"I don't think so."

"So say it already!"

"OK! After prom it's over." Lisa blurts.

"Wait. What? What do you mean? What are you talking about?"

"It's over. I like you, but I need something better. I need more."

"Better like what? More what?" Derrick is confused.

"You're just good enough and I want someone who is going to be better." Lisa explains.

"Be better? Make it?" Derrick scoffs. "Do you understand that I have a full ride to school plus job offers already lined up?"

"Yes but I just don't see it. Besides, I'm sorry I have a new boyfriend," Lisa confesses. "He can take care of all my needs. He's much older than us."

"What needs? You are barely out of school."

"But I want a baby and you are all like let's wait and all that. You're just too much of a good boy."

"So basically. You want someone that is going to use and abuse you? This person has obviously got your head wrapped around some dumb shit," Derrick says angrily. "Why in the hell you can't wait. We have planned our lives and all of a sudden you just change your mind. Are you serious?"

"I do love you and all but still. This is what I want now and you can't give it to me."

"I can give you that and more. We just have to wait a little bit."

"Yeah in four years. I don't want to be too old starting a family."

"You'll only be like 22."

"You just don't get it…"

"You know what screw it," Derrick screams and throws his hand up in the air like his father does. "I ain't going to prom with you. Have your *man* take you."

Derrick opens his eyes and the tears begin to run down his face. He continues to wonder "what-if". The pit of his stomach is in knots. He stands up and grabs the beer he sat down on the table. He walks into the kitchen and turns on the stove. He stands there looking at the picture one final time before placing it on the burner. The smoke alarm goes off and he just stands there.

Reflection: Alana

Alana left Finley and Alex at the Coroner's Office. She's in the car and the music is blaring loud. Oddly enough "Bad Boys" by Bob Marley is playing on the radio. She smiles thinking of how she got started in all of this. She used to role play all the time with her friends. She was very happy that they were just as weird as her.

Alana walks up in her police costume that she got for Halloween.

"So what do we got?" She asks with authority.

Unlike now, Jason was smaller than Alana. Even then they were partners fighting crime.

"Well detective," Jason replied playing along. "As you can see we got a dead body on our hands."

(Another teen girl is lying stiff in the grass. They have outlined her in chalk.)

"OK M.E. notified?" Alana asked.

"Yes Ma'am. It looks as if she fell out the window." Jason points up at the open window.

"Uh huh." (Everyone looks up at the window on the second floor open with the curtain flying out. Derrick waives.) "Suicide is definitely not it."

"Why do you say that?"

"Look at the glass around her and how the window is shattered."

"Right."

"This is definitely foul play. Any witnesses?"

"Neighbors say they heard arguing."

"Did they see anyone come or go?"

"The only thing they saw was a figure. But they couldn't say whether or not it was a man or woman."

"Let's go back and see if we can get any more details."

"Yes ma'am."

"Look at that. Her leg is in an awkward position for an accident or even suicide."

They all look up from the dead body as Alana's father pulls up in the driveway. Everyone says hello in unison once he is out of the car. He looks on in amazement. He smiles then goes into cop mode.

"And how are you?" (Looking at the girl on the ground.) Mr. Wells asks.

"Dead. How do you think I am?"

"Suicide?"

"No. Besides dead people really don't talk."

"Well actually they do you just have to listen harder."

The kids look on like he is about to perform a séance.

He turns to Alana. "Any leads?"

"I have a pretty good idea." She responds.

"Go with your instincts. 9 times out 10, your first thought is the correct thought," Her dad says. "Even if it seems farfetched and out of the ordinary."

"10-4. Roger that!"

Alana salutes her father. He kisses her gently on the forehead. Then he steps over the dead body.

All the kids gasps and he shoots them a "yeah I did look". He looks down at the young girl on the ground and he winks his eye. She giggles.

Day dreaming almost gets Wells killed. She ran the light and barely missed oncoming traffic. She speeds up in just enough time. As she slows she flashes her badge around her neck to the cop running traffic on the other side of the street. He nods, but gives her a stern look. She remains focused as she reaches the courthouse.

In the Judge's Chambers

Wells walks into the courthouse confident that she is doing the right thing. There is a pungent smell. Normally it smells like a sanitized hospital but today it's not that. Someone must have gotten some bad news. She now wishes she hadn't eaten at all today. She wants to throw up herself. She continues to the judge's chamber. For her, time is of the essence for so many reasons. She knocks on the door.

Judge Givens is sitting at his desk looking over some papers.

"Come in."

"Good afternoon Your Honor. Thank you for seeing me on such short notice."

"Do you understand what you are asking me?"

"Yes sir. I fully do and I believe that this will help the case."

"I am not sure I can honor all of your requests. "

"Your honor, we have four homicides and no leads. I need to do an autopsy on these people. Besides don't you think it's kind of odd that none of them asked for an autopsy? I would think it was needed for insurance purposes."

"People have different reasons for requesting not to have one done. Religious, political or whatever. Besides, what will this prove?

"Honestly, I don't know but it's all I have left."

"This is something I have to think on."

"I understand Your Honor but time is money and of the essence and I don't have a lot of it left."

"I admire your spirit. I will have a decision for you by this evening."

"Thank you sir. I understand sir."

She stands up, shakes his hand and leaves. She smirks as she is never one to back down from a fight. Well at least at the moment when she wanted to jet out to Cape Verde. She needs a vacation so it felt like the opportune time. She heads back to the station to see if Finley made it back. She totally forgot that she left him at the morgue with Alex. Alex, how she wanted him so bad right now. Maybe later she will call and see if he's still mad. So what. She would have him - mad or not.

Word has gotten to media and they are swarming the place. Wells is bombarded with questions.

Reporter One: "Is it true that even your father can't solve these cases?"

Reporter Two: "What is like to have four homicides with no link and no clues?"

Reporter Three: "Do you think you'll ever figure this out?"

Reporter Four: "What is the police station doing to assist you?"

Reporter Five: "Is it true you are sleeping with the M.E. and your judgment is clouded?"

She stops short on that question. In all honesty since that day she has actually been thinking much clearer. However, she will not be speaking on that. They are continuing to throw questions at her and at this point she's not sure if she wants to answer any of them. It gets to be overwhelming. Wells grabs her head and pushes her way to the police station door. They continue to follow her asking questions. She hasn't even given them a "no comment". Her father is there to bail her out like usual.

She heads towards her desk. Finley is sitting there and he doesn't know whether to be mad or give her a good slap on the back. He has this Cheshire cat smile on his face with a piece of paper in his hand. She's trying to ignore her father wondering why Finley is all grins.

Adam slows her pace to have a private conversation.

"OK honey so – you are right. I have played that scene back and forth and I have nothing."

(Smirking and raising an eyebrow.) "Oh you don't say?"

"What do you have planned? Finley is closed lipped about something. I swear he's a sneaky one. Whatever that paper is, he's waiting for you."

"Nothing yet." She walks away.

Wells turns her attention to Finley.

"So how did it go?"

"Don't know. I'm supposed to hear something by the end of the day. Wait. You already know! Give me that!"

"Do you think it will work?"

"Don't know. I really hope so. But poor daddy over there doesn't know what to do with himself. I'm for sure am not giving him any ideas or a taste of what I know. Maybe ever."

"No way. Alana being defiant towards her father? This is a first!"

"Yes way. It's time for 'daddy' to respect who I am. I AM the lead detective on this case. He's the hired help."

"I hope you are doing this for the better good. Well not so much for him but the families?"

"Exactly. I'm just glad the good judge came through."

"Imagine that – a judge with some morals."

"Hey! Watch it. Someone hears that and it could cause trouble."

"It's just a joke."

"Well not all jokes are accepted. Let's go to *Daddy's* crime scene."

"Yes sir!"

How the Other Half Live

It is well into the evening. The sun has set and it has a beautiful hue of orange, red, purple and green. It is amazing Wells thinks. She stares out as Finley drives. He took the keys. There is no way she's leaving him stranded again if she doesn't get her way. They pull into an elaborate driveway. By the looks of Mr. Lingerman's home, it has already made him apprehensive. Hopefully they are not as stuffy as their house looks overpriced.

They get out of the car simultaneously and stare at each other. They walk up to the door and Wells rings the doorbell. The butler answers the door. He's stuffy. He looks upon them as if they are asking for charity. Immediately Wells attitude has risen. Finley looks at her left hand as she balls it in a fist. He steps up a little closer to protect them - him from getting hurt and her from losing her job.

"May I help you?" Maybe it was just her, but the butler sounded so arrogant.

Wells is really taken back by his presence.

"Uh, um, hi, I'm Detective Wells and this is Finley. We are here to see Mr. Lingerman."

"The authorities have been here already several times and Mr. Lingerman is not in the mood to speak with anyone. We do not need the press pretending to be something they are not."

Wells pushes her way inside. The butler is surprised she has so much strength.

"Uh well that's too bad cause see I have another dead woman on my hands and well (looking around) considering that's his wife, I think I'll speak to him (looking directly into his eyes) anyway."

"You know I'd do as she says. She has this temper you wouldn't believe and on top of that – you could go to jail for hindering an investigation."

(In disgust) "One moment please – have a seat."(He gestures toward the elegant sofa and walks away.)

Alana scoffs. "Wow. Yeah he's shook up alright."

"He's just hired help."

"Yeah, well. We might have a lead. Think. Fancy house. Big bills. Money tight. Insurance policy, maybe?

"Nah. I don't think so."

"Where are the grieving people? Why is the house so in order?"

"Hired help. Their job is to keep the house in order."

"I'm telling you. I'm not feeling it. My aunt died and we had people over for weeks. This here is eerie. Not one person to visit? Not even her family?"

"Maybe he likes the quiet. Sometimes people do respect your wishes. Guy like this; I wouldn't cross him. So why are we back here?"

"I got a little something but I'm not sure at the moment. I need some time and feel him out."

"Really?"

"No one sees it and I can't say without proof."

"That whole farfetched thing huh?"

"Sadly. Yeah."

(Wells face looks a little sad. Finley notices it.)

"Penny for your thoughts? Oh wait make that like a twenty. I forgot you are all educated and stuff."

(Slight laugh.) "Nothing. Just thinking."

"Must be some deep thought."

In walks Mr. Lingerman.

(There is a drink in hand and grief in his face.) "Yes? How may I help you detectives?"

"Mr. Lingerman, I'm Wells and this is Finley. I know many people have spoken with you and it's all over the news, but I would like to ask you a few more questions if that is ok?"

"I'm quite sure. Considering you drove all the way over here. Would you like anything to drink?"

Finley raises a hand. "No thank you. We have a strict no drinking on the job policy. Although I get off at 10:00 and can come back and take you up on that offer."

(Laughs really hard.) "Thank you. That was nice. I hadn't laughed since my wife's passing."

"Well. (He shrugs his shoulders.) It wasn't a joke but ok."

(Alana looks sternly at Finley.) "Well let's get down to business. First, where did you find your wife?"

"As I have told everyone else, in the pool."

"And the butler?"

"Was out on errands."

"Convenient."

"Actually more like routine. He takes care of house business every Wednesday."

"Okay. I wonder though. You sure she was *in* the pool?"

"Her clothes were wet and she was floating in the pool. I assumed that she was out for a swim."

"The problem I'm having with this is that you waited like 2 or 3 hours." Alana furrows her brows in concern. "In addition, she was not in the normal swim attire. That did not strike you as odd?"

"Yes, she loves to swim and so it's nothing for her to stay out there for hours. So I just did some work on the computer. When I looked up she was still in the same spot. That's when I went out to see if she was ok. And she wasn't."

"So she drowned?"

"As with the others. It was cause unknown."

"When is the funeral?"

"We have already had it."

At that moment a beautiful and vivacious young woman uses a key to let herself into the house. All eyes focus on her. She is dressed quite scandalous and yet professional at the same time. Her slender legs even has Finley licking his lips as if she were a perfect steak ready to be devoured. She looks over startled. Her name is Stacey. Secretly she may have something going on with Mr. Lingerman.

"Mr. Lingerman. I'm sorry. I did not know you had company."

"That is okay. Can you please go grab those reports and look them over until I can finish with the detectives?"

"But of course. I do apologize for interrupting."

"That's okay. Thank you."

She quickly exits the room.

Finley can't resist. "Personal at home secretarial service who has her own key?"

"Why yes. Stacey has been with the company since she was 16. She just graduated with her Master's Degree and has been promoted. I trust her. Besides when I'm out of town she checks on my wife and gets things for me."

Wells is feeling a little disappointed - "Oh okay. Well Mr. Lingerman thank you for your time. I may need to ask you a few more questions but of course it won't be unannounced as in today. I just had to get away from the station."

"Yes. I have seen you on TV."

She chuckles. "So I guess I'm a little famous huh?"

Mr. Lingerman stands up to escort them to the door. "Well, yes detective. Until we meet again." He bows and kisses her hand.

At that very moment she wanted nothing more but to go up to his room and see what he was made of.

"Thank you."

Finley quickly glances at his partner and longtime friend. He's not sure of what to make of her at this time.

It's a new day and the city moves forward. The news reporters are still left to speculate what is going on as no one is speaking to them. **They** *are not pleased. Therefore no one is safe.* **They** *are in the basement. It is very, very dark. There is the sound of dripping water. The gentleman's breathing is quite labored and panicked.*

Sitting in a chair is an elderly man. He appears to be wet. There is residue all around him and over him. He is tied to electrical wires. The electricity is cracking and the wires are glowing.

They: *(In a whisper.)* "Do you know how many volts it takes to kill a human? *(Angrily.)* Do you know? Oh, I'm quite sure you do. You've seen executions before. Yeah, considering who you are. Thanks to you... I think you know. My question is about to be answered for you though."

They throw the switch. The gentleman's body starts to seize. His eyes bulge as he stares into his killers eyes. It is over as quickly as it started.

In the News

Wells is in her apartment. She is wearing lounging clothes drinking coffee. The news is on in the background. As much as she wants to drown it out, she keeps it on. It is worse than keeping the police scanner on all night. She walks towards the kitchen when something catches her ear.

Male anchor person: "In the latest breaking story, Dale Parsons, an outstanding citizen, leader and Professor at Colorado State University was found dead in his home at approximately 06:30am." (Her phone rings – her heart skips a beat.) "As with the latest killings police have no leads, no motive and this has turned into any police officer's worst nightmare – a serial killer. We are joined live by Teresa Bills at the scene."

Teresa Bills is an upcoming news reporter and this is her first live reporting. Her facial expressions are nothing short of nervousness. There is an even more pregnant pause than usual in her reaction time. She is snapped into place by the camera man and she begins. It is raining and they are standing across the street in front of Dale Parsons' home.

"Thank you. Many neighbors are saying that no one saw or heard anything. They are devastated. As this is such a cruel thing. He was a kind gentleman and he always spoke words of influence. I personally know Mr. Parsons as I have had several classes with him. I am truly overcome by this tragedy as with all tragedies. Who could have done such a horrible thing? Right now police are trying to gather as much information as possible and follow any leads. Unfortunately, there are none. The only thing they are saying is for people to take precaution because there is no real link to any of the victims and it appears to be random. Back to you Chad."

"Thank you."

In Teresa's ear her producer gives her a tongue lashing of a lifetime.

"What the hell was that?! Are you kidding me?!"

"Hey, it just happened ok?"

"Well you can kiss your career good-bye. As your just happened was live and no station is going to want an "off the cuff", pausing reporter. Don't let it happen again. Just report the facts. Or there won't be a next time."

"Sure. OK. I apologize. This time."

In between the news cast, Wells is getting dressed and you can hear her irritation. "I'm getting dressed now. I know. I know. Look - I'll be there."

She Explodes

The rain has not let up. It is pouring out. She is irritated already as this is her first day off in weeks and she was called in. Not to mention she has not made up with Alex yet and she is really longing for his touch right now. Today would have been a perfect day. Instead her mood is foul and she is not in the mood for anything or anyone.

There is much clamor as she is walking into the police station. As she walked up her aura must have been felt as not one reporter threw one question to her. She walks over to her desk and slams everything down. She is not there a good five minutes before the Chief walks up to her and starts in on her. Finley does not move, his mouth is open and he is trying to decide if he even wants to get in the middle of it.

(The Chief is very angry. To the point he is yelling.) "You gotta get a hold on this and pretty damn quick! I am up to my ass in reporters and the mayor wants to know what in the hell is going on? I am at my wits ends with you and your father. You're supposed to be the best of the best!"

"Hold on! I didn't claim to be anything! I do my job and that's it! I didn't ask for these cases. YOU gave them to me! If it was any other officer, would you be this way? Hell no. SO BACK OFF! Last I recall you told me to close the case as unsolved. Now that your ass is in a sling you want to jump all over me? To hell with you!"

"Excuse me? I am your superior."

"Well right now – you ain't that super."

"Watch yourself Wells. I'll…"

"What?! Take me off the case? Fire me?" (Rolling her eyes.) "You'd be doing me a favor."

"You are really pushing it!"

"No what's pushing it is you going behind my back and asking my father to step in. How dare you! Friend or not – you know better than to have another detective step in on a case and not inform them. What kind of Chief are you?"

At this point everything stops or seems to. No one has ever stood up or talked back to the Chief the way Alana is right now. There are plenty of open mouths. Total shock. So much so even the people being booked are quiet.

"I'm the kind of Chief who depended on you and you failed."

"What?! Did you just…" (She lunges forward at the Chief and Finley jumps to her side to defend her and pull her back.) "You know what?" (She takes a deep breath.) "Thanks. I'm done!"

"What do you mean you're done?"

He now realizes the gravity of his actions and his words.

(Disarming herself - very sternly.) "It means, I quit – you can have it – find yourself another detective. As a matter of fact why don't you get Finley to take over! He's been playing second chair for a while and he's just as good as anyone else because I am out of here!"

As she speaks these words her father walks through the door and Finley jumps up again. Adam looks for the first time like an embarrassed father. The tension in the air is very thick. Finley is the first to speak.

"Whoa. Now hold on, hold on, hold on. First of all I don't WANT these cases. Second of all I like second chair and third of all you can't quit!" (He looks and points to her father.)

"Wanna bet? I should not have taken this job at all. It's too stressful. Besides, he really doesn't matter anymore."

"Not the person who can handle anything. Are you sure."

"No going back Finley. Yes I am. This takes the cake."

"Let me buy you some cookies then cause ain't no way you givin' this to me."

"Don't worry my *daddy* can help you out." (She points to Adam and storms out.)

"Something's up." Adam looks at Chief Williams.

"You don't say."

It is still raining outside and she is glad because she didn't want anyone to see her crying. She walks swiftly to her car. She falls to the ground crying uncontrollably. She doesn't bother to see if anyone is looking and she lets out a scream that has come from a deep and dark place. For that second – it felt good to let everything go. She gets in her car to phone Derrick.

Derrick is sitting on the couch. He is reading over the latest stats. He takes a sip of his coffee when the phone rings.

"Hello?"

"Hey it's me."

"Hey baby how you doing?"

"How do you think?"

"Where are you?"

"In the car soaked and wet."

"Why?"

"I just quit my job and I don't know what to do."

"Well baby, do you want to come over. Yeah?"

"Yeah."

"See you in a few."

"Mmm K."

The drive is normally 30 minutes, but today it feels longer. She pulls up in the driveway. She hesitates momentarily before getting out of the car. She decides that since she is there; she might as well. She walks in soaked. He grabs her and holds her close.

"You okay."

"No. I'm lost."

"Not the famous detective."

"I guess I'm gonna get even more popular by quitting and leaving those cases open."

"Do you feel comfortable with your decision?"

"I guess."

"Then don't second guess yourself."

"I don't know. I guess I do feel better now that I'm with you."

"Of course, you can always stay with me. I never get tired of you."

"I know I can always count on you."

Derrick leans over and kisses her passionately on the lips. She returns the kiss and leads him to the shower. A part of her still wishes she was with Alex. This is the very reason she does not get into relationships or make commitments. She is a free spirit and having whom she wants when she wants is who she is. Feelings cannot be a part of the arrangement. Shortly thereafter, Derrick & Alana are lying in bed holding each other.

"And you are sure this is going to work," asks Derrick as he holds her hand.

"As sure as I have ever been."

"No one knows who's behind all this?"

"No one has a clue."

"What about your father?"

"Considering he's *not really* my father. I'd say it's all good."

"And your mother?"

"Well, that will be a tough one, but hey I'm in it to win it."

"Do you love me?"

"Eh. Somewhat." She laughs a teasingly laugh but Derrick is unsure of how to feel.

Deep down he really loves her, but he's not sure how far she'd be willing to go. She really just may be the death of him.

She falls asleep quickly.

Dreaming of Terry

Derrick falls asleep just as quickly. These have been trying times for the both of them. He tosses and turns dreaming... Dreaming of Terry.

It was a splendid afternoon. The kind of afternoon that made him want to call in sick for work. The only thing is that Lingerman Technologies is his life. Plus there was the team meeting that he couldn't miss.

Mr. Lingerman is grinning from ear to ear. "Well team, I brought you together to give you the latest numbers. The D.O.D. just signed US a $30M dollar check for a job well done. We are up in stocks by 15% and approvals from D.O.D. is at an all-time high of 94.7% and for that expect bonuses for each member! How does that sound?"

Team agrees and shouts different accolades.

"And, and – because of her outstanding job performance, Terry Shaw is now Team Leader 2 and will head up the next project. I expect great things from you." (Looking over at Terry.)

Terry gasps in excitement. "Oh." Terry is a rather slender young woman, light in complexion, long hair and brown eyes. She has dimples when she smiles.

Derrick clears his throat. "Well Mr. Lingerman, I think I would be better suited for the project seeing that I'm TL1. That will require long hours and extensive testing."

"All of which is why I'm giving this to her. I think this will be the perfect breakout for her. Don't worry DW she's not out for your job. She's looking for a team of her own. Now ain't that right little Miss?"

Terry is still stunned. "Why of course. I mean. That's uh. Wow!"

"Well now I will need more than 1, 2, 3 word sentences; that way I know you can handle things. I'm happy to see that you are on board."

Derrick looks with approval and yet is concerned. Everyone leaves. Derrick & Terry stands there looking at each other. She screams and jumps in his arms.

"Oh my God Baby! Can you believe it?! This is amazing."

Derrick gently slides her to the table and is standing in between her legs. "Baby, I am no doubt proud of you. You work so hard all the time. It's just that I'm concerned about..."

"Little Derrick? Or Derricka?"

"Now that's not funny." He chuckles.

"See Baby, (grabbing his face) everything is going to be okay. We're getting married in a few weeks and then I'll be out of your hair. All of our plans and goals are coming together. Besides, mostly we will have the same hours. PLUS, it'll do us some good to have a little space between us so that we don't get tired of each other."

"I could never tire of you. I look into those beautiful brown eyes and I lose the world. I find peace with you."

"Well, let's see if you can find my lips because I need a celebratory kiss."

He kisses her long, deep and passionately. Forgetting that they are both at work.

Later on that evening at Derrick's place. The fireplace is lit with candles all around. Derrick and Terry are lying in front of the fireplace. Derrick is holding Terry and rubbing her stomach.

Terry purrs and stretches like a kitten. "MMMMMMMM That feels sooo good."

"I think I spoil you too much."

"That's okay, I'm supposed to be spoiled. Really."

Derrick laughs. "Oh really?"

"Yes really. It's in the Pregnant Baby Momma Handbook. Did you not get your copy? It's right next to 'What to Expect When Expecting'."

"Humph. No, I guess I must've missed that one. I'll have to check it out."

Terry in a deep voice. "Oh yeah." Then back to her normal voice. "It's on page 32 right next to going to the store for late night cravings."

Derrick hangs his head in shame. He knows what *that* means) "Oh no."

"Oh come on Baby. I hardly ever really ask for anything."

"I know. I know." (Getting up.) "Why can't you have normal cravings like ice cream and pickles?"

"That's sooo cliché you know."

"I guess. Can I get me something too? Or is this one of your selfish nights."

"Oh. No. No. You can get whatever you please. You're paying!"

"Anything I want?" (Stroking her inner thigh.) "Since, I'm paying and all."

"Well *that's* gonna cost ya a little more than that."

"Let me check my 401K."

"That and the pension Baby. Now go." She pushes him towards the door - he stumbles and they both laugh heartily.

Terry's cell phone rings.

Derrick opens the door and glancing back. "Don't get that." He closes the door behind him.

Terry looks at the phone. "Hello?"

Tech #1: "Hey Terry. Sorry to bother you on your night off but we have a situation. We are missing 3 canisters and the tests are off by 20%."

"What happened because when I left yesterday, I was off by only 11%?"

Tech #1: "I don't know, but Mr. L was here and he blew 2 head gaskets. His face was redder than the ripest tomato. He said that if we don't get this fixed by tomorrow morning – we all will be on the soup line. And I don't particularly like soup."

"No time for jokes. Ugh! He's gonna be so pissed. I'm on my way. **FIND THOSE TESTS!**"

She hangs up before getting a response. She looks for the pen and pad. Scribbles a quick note letting Derrick know where she was. She writes, *Love Me Some U*, blows out the candles, and runs out the door. Meanwhile Derrick makes it to the corner grocery store. The cashier Hannah Cain recognizes him right away and she smiles.

She has a distorted face. She reminds him of Terry when she sees something she doesn't like. "Does she actually *eat* all that?"

"Yes and sometimes she makes me eat it with her."

"Wow, you are a good man. Got any brothers, uncles, cousins, friends, neighbors, friends of friends, nephews or in laws? Really, I'm not that picky."

Derrick laughs. "None that would be good enough for you."

"I mean you gotta know somebody right? Would she mind you having two wives? You know in some cultures you can have up to four."

"You know what? If she wasn't a chemical specialist and I didn't fear for my life – I would think about it. Besides, my heart is for only one other woman outside of my mother."

He caresses her face, pays for the groceries purchased and leaves the change as a tip and walks out. Driving in his car, Derrick turns on the radio headed home and hears Celine Dion "Because You Love Me". He smiles – thinking of how that's the song they will marry to. He gets home and sees that most of the lights are out. Typical. She asks for something and then goes to sleep.

Derrick opens the door - in the worst Ricky Ricardo voice - "Lucy, I'm home." There is no response. "Terry? Terry?" He walks toward the table, sets down the bags on the table and heads over to the bathroom. He knocks on the door. "Terry?"

He walks back into the Living Room. He looks around and sees the note on the table. Reads it and gets angry but looks at the bottom at the Love Me Some U and smiles. At the bottom he sees the, *P.S. Don't Get Mad.*

Terry is entering the lab. Speaking to Tech #1. It is about 11:30pm.

"Yo! What's the deal?"

"I got us down to 13% but as for those files. We still can't locate them."

"Who signed out last?"

Tech #2 checks the log: "T.J. did."

"Where's T.J.?"

Tech #2: "I assumed he went home for the day."

"Did you check his office?"

Tech #1: "I did but it was locked."

"OK. Let's worry about that later. I'm quite sure he has it." (Yawns.) "Let me see if I can remember what I did."

Terry is looking over papers. The techs have all walked over to other desks. The time is passing and she grows even more tired. She rubs her stomach. She begins to pull out flasks and tubes and mixing chemicals. She does not notice that she has pulled the wrong flask and pours. There is a quick flash and plenty of smoke. Once the alarms go off - they run over with masks to Terry who has fallen to the ground.

Tech #1 pulls the knob for ventilation and the smoke clears – they find Terry only she is not breathing. Tech #2 runs to get the first aid kit and begin CPR. Tech #1 goes over to the phone and dials 911. Once he hangs up from EMS – he calls Derrick to give him the news.

Derrick is lying in the bed watching television. The phone rings. He looks at the Caller ID." Why hello beautiful. I thought you forgot about me."

Tech#1: Um, Derrick this is John.

He leans forward. Sternly - "Why are you calling me?"

"There's been an accident."

"What kind of accident."

"We were off and missing some files. So I called Terry to get her help." He hesitates before speaking again. "We were at our desks and she was making the mix again and she mixed the wrong chemicals."

Derrick begins to cry and sob. "Oh God! No! Why in the hell did you call her? I would have been there in the morning!"

"But Mr. Lingerman..."

"Damn that! Where is she?"

"They took her to the hospital but..."

"Shut up."

He hangs up, quickly gets dressed and leaves.

The morning comes and the sun is shining, but today feels like such a gloomy day. Derrick is in the waiting room – pacing. Alana is with him. The doctor walks in. There is such a look of melancholy on his face that Alana has seen too many times before. She holds her breath as he speaks.

"Derrick?"

Derrick rushes over to the doctor. "Yes?" (Alana quickly stands behind him.)

The doctor has tears in his eyes. That's a first – Alana thinks.

"I'm so sorry. We did everything we could."

"I know her, but the baby?"

The doctor bows his head. His voice barely audible. "No. Whatever the chemical mix was… It was so strong and quick that it travelled to the baby's blood stream and we couldn't save him."

"Him?"

Alana lets out a loud – "Oh God."

At that point Derrick falls to the ground. She stoops next to him when her tears begin to fall. She looks to the doctor.

"They didn't know the sex. It was a surprise. They didn't know."

"Oh God. I'm so sorry. I'm so sorry."

Terry's face flashes before Derrick's eyes. Then an image of her holding their son and smiling. It is such a beautiful smile that would melt the heart. He reaches for her and the baby and they disappear. He screams so loud and there are loud sobs. He becomes so uncontrollable and in consolable that the doctor motions for a sedative and immediately he passes out.

Derrick gasps and sits up. Almost crying. "Terry?"

Alana recognizes quickly he must have been dreaming. She calmly and soothingly speaks - "No, it's me Alana."

His crying is very prevalent now. "I miss her so much."

"I know." (She sits up and wraps her arms around him.) "I do too. She was a sweet person."

"Was? She is."

"Derrick. You have to be strong. She needs you to be strong for her. As long as you feel her – she will always be with you."

"Thank God for you." (He squeezes her tight.) "I don't know what I would do without you."

"Mm Hmm. I know." (She kisses his cheek.) "You just wouldn't make it."

She rolls back over to sleep. Her bare back is showing and Derrick just stares at how beautiful she is.

Mom is Concerned

Adam is sitting at the kitchen table drinking a cup of coffee. He is talking to Cynthia and she has a look of worry mixed with anger in her face. She is worried that her kids are losing it and angry at Adam for pushing them so hard.

"So she just quit?"

"Just like that. I was walking through the door and saw the whole thing. She and the Chief were into it big and one thing led to another."

She turns to fully face him and stares him square in the eye. "And you don't think you played a part in that?"

"What?"

"What my ass. You basically told her that she was not doing a good job - *her job* and that she was embarrassing the great Adam Wells. You do it all the time and to step in and take over HER case? What were you thinking?"

"Williams called me. I didn't call him."

"Right and you didn't think about the ramifications from that? I mean really?!" (She lets out a sigh of defeat.) "Finley called and warned that she's going to Cape Verde and may not come back."

"Has she called?"

"NO!"

"Then where is she?"

"I don't know. I've been calling her and Derrick and neither one are answering."

"I'll go by his place. They must be together. This is a hard time for the both of them."

"I know, the baby would be born today."

"My first grand baby. Man, it must be hard. That's probably why they aren't answering."

(Speaking very sternly as with any concerned mother would be.) "Either way - find out what's going on with my babies."

"I will." He gets up to leave when the phone rings.

"Hello?" She glances over at Adam and reaches to give him the phone. "It's for you."

"Yeah. Hey, Williams. Are you kidding me? When? What? Okay, I'm on my way anyway." He grabs his coat – kisses Cynthia and leaves.

"Hey!" (He turns to face her.) "Get a hold of my babies!"

Adam nods in agreement.

Old Habits Die Hard

Alana is at her apartment – she's getting dressed. She contemplates whether or not she made the right decision as she glances over at the stacks of paper on her desk. She still has copies of all the files. She walks over and stares at them. She finally picks them up after what seems like the longest two minutes of her life. There is something familiar about them all but she's really not placing it. The look on her face says that she is very close. She grabs her phone to call Finley.

Finley is at the station sitting at his desk. He stares at Well's desk in amazement that she gave up. This is his best friend. The only partner he has ever had. He gets a sinking feeling knowing that in a few short minutes Adam will be walking through that door to totally take over. This is not the Wells he would like to deal with. He needs that spunky go-getter that has nothing to lose but everything to gain. His dress is a little more casual. There's no need to try if he's not standing next to the hottest detective on the force.

The phone rings. He snaps out of his daydream.

"Finley."

"Hey, Fins."

"Well. So you do remember who your friends are."

"Ha, ha. Yep – I guess so. Hey, listen, can you meet me at our spot?"

"Is this a date because you know it's no longer business between us?"

"Um, no but I think I may have something to help you with the cases."

He takes a deep sigh. "Well, I would love to meet you however, there's a slight problem."

"Oh, yeah, what's that?"

"Oh let's add another one to the case?"

"Huh?"

"Yep. Call came in just a few minutes ago and we're just waiting on Daddy Wells to get here. This time the scene is fresh. May even have a witness."

"Wow."

"See what you've been missing?" He pauses.

"What is it?" Alana asks knowing when her partner is silent there is something.

"This one is weird though."

"Weird how?"

"It's a homeless person."

She's puzzled. "A homeless person?"

"Yeah."

"And how do you know this is one and the same?"

"The killer left a note."

"Bull."

"Yep. So the Chief's all over this."

"That can't be. It's a copycat."

"I thought so too, but I got the feeling that this isn't over and well; someone needs to explain why the D.O.D. is here."

"The D.O.D.? No way."

"Yep. Department of Defense, Center for Disease Control, National Space Agency. They're probably tapping the lines as we speak. Maybe to see if there a mole or something. This is bigger than we thought. You picked the wrong time to leave darling. Now Daddy gets all the glory."

"OK so something's up. I believe that. That's why you gotta get me as much info as you can, you know, and meet me so we can talk."

"Just show up at the crime scene like usual. I guarantee no one will notice."

"OK where?"

"The corner of Colfax and Spear."

"OK I'll be there. Does anyone know what the note says?"

"Yeah, 'let's take this to the next level.'"

"Next level?"

"Yep. What level that is – I don't know."

"Actually, I need to go see someone. Just get some info for me and call me later."

"Roger that."

Is Big Brother in Trouble

It is midafternoon now and Alana decided go to Lingerman Technologies to visit her brother. There is much clamor and whispering. Derrick is looking calm yet concerned. Mr. Lingerman is talking with the team. He is very upset. At the same time the look of concern on his face says everything. He knows what this leak could potentially do to the business. Not to mention the millions he will lose.

Mr. Lingerman takes a deep breath, "Who leaked it?"

Derrick averts his eyes. This is the first time he does not look Mr. Lingerman in the eye. "No one to my knowledge."

"Do we know if the media has been around, called or anything?"

John hesitates, "no."

Derrick turns to fully face the team, "What in the world is going on here?"

Mr. Lingerman steps forward, "Where are the files?"

John turns around and grabs a stack of papers, "all of the files are accounted for."

Mr. Lingerman steps closer to Derrick – barely a whisper – "Derrick, could anyone have made copies?"

"Not to my knowledge."

Mr. Lingerman raises an eyebrow – "T.J.?"

"No not T.J. He wouldn't, let alone couldn't, do anything like that. He knew what this meant."

"Well, I know the authorities will be here soon. So let's get your statements together."

On cue, Alana walks in. Everyone stops and stares at her as if she was a model and she is in a runway show. The atmosphere changes slightly.

She looks toward Mr. Lingerman and smiles. "Why hello Mr. Lingerman."

Derrick looks up. That was the most sultry and sexy voice he has heard from her in a very long time. He frowns so deeply that it catches her eye. She winks at him and stands directly in front of Mr. Lingerman. She places out her hand. Derrick really gets frazzled by the gesture. Deep inside his blood is boiling. He anticipates what is to happen next.

Mr. Lingerman coyly smiles back. "Why Ms. Wells, what a pleasure to see you again." They shake hands and Derrick exhales. Mr. Lingerman pauses to think. "Wait is this about what's been going on?"

She shoots him a look as if she has no clue of what he is referring to. "Uh, no. I'm just here to see that handsome devil over there." (Nodding towards Derrick. He smiles.) "Can I steal him for a moment?"

"How do you two know each other?"

"Why Mr. Lingerman – you can't tell." (Smiles.)

"Are you dating?"

Derrick bubbles over. "Wow, now how freaky would that be to date your sister?"

Mr. Lingerman blushes. "I – forgive me – I never put the two together. Besides Derrick, as close as I thought we were, I didn't know you had a sister."

"Yep. I have one. Didn't want one." (He walks over to Alana and wraps his arm around her waist.) "But, I'm glad she here. I guess."

Alana scoffs at the idea of what he just said. "Well, I need some alone time with you."

"Sure. Excuse me Mr. Lingerman, I'll only be a moment."

Mr. Lingerman smiles with a fatherly approval. "Why sure."

As they walk out, Alana turns back with a flirty smile. "Thanks." Mr. Lingerman waves a hand.

John fumbles for words, "Hey Alana."

"Hey!"

Inside Derrick chuckles because he knows that "hey". That's the "I don't want to be bothered hey, I don't like you hey, why are you talking to me hey, I'm only speaking to be polite hey" or what she likes to call the "fake hey" all wrapped up in that chipper hey as if he just mattered if only for that moment.

They walk down the long hallway to Derrick's office. They don't speak until they are in the office. She always wondered whether or not if the building ever got dirty. For as long as she could remember, the building was in immaculate condition. Derrick's office is no exception, which she could say more about his room. His office is filled with cabinets and files. The periodic table covers one side of the wall. There are plenty of pictures of Alana and Terry all around. His office is a mess however, strangely, it is neat at the same time.

Derrick closes the door. "What's up?"

(She hugs him very tightly.)

OK. What was that for?"

"You know that I love you with all my heart right?"

Derrick smiles deeply. "From the ground to the sky right?"

Alana smiles, but tears fill her eyes. "Yes. Of course."

"OK baby. You are scaring me."

"I want you to come to Cape Verde with me."

Derrick is taken back. There is surprise in his voice. "Oh. I can't. I have a lot going on here."

"I know and that's why I want you to come with me."

"I'm confused."

She becomes a little stern. "Derrick, I know."

"You know what?"

"I know all about what's going on here."

Derrick looks very concerned. He sits on the edge of his desk and crosses his arms. "Be straight forward. What exactly *do* you *know*?"

Alana starts sobbing. "I know about the murders and everything. I put some of it together but I haven't gotten it all, but it won't be long before everyone else figures it out too." (She begs him.) "Please come with me?"

"Wait, you think that somehow, *I'm* linked to this?"

"I saw the files. Since when did you bring work home? I have to admit that I was impressed at first but now... I just can't lose you."

"First of all. I'm not going anywhere. Second, I felt something was going on BUT I can guarantee. It's not me."

"I don't know."

"What do you mean 'you don't know'? You gotta believe me."

"I want to but where were you last night?"

"What do you mean?"

"For about 45 minutes or so you weren't in the bed with me. I assumed that maybe you went for a walk or was in the restroom, something but…"

"I was in the living room. I didn't want to disturb you considering. Right now, I've been feeling differently. My baby, Terry – you know. I had the work with me because I was trying to see what happened that night. Why did it have to be her? Am I angry yes but I'm no serial killer. NOR would I do this to Mr. Lingerman."

"Well, it's gonna be linked to you. I've done this for far too long and you know they gotta have someone to pin this on and right now the only person I see is you."

"Wait, whoa, whoa, whoa. Wait. Why me?"

"You kinda got a motive. The most important one is losing your family."

"True, but that's not enough."

"It doesn't take much to set you off so. My offer stands. I leave next Friday. You have until Wednesday to answer me. And think about this, do you really want Daddy to arrest his own son?"

Derrick sits there contemplating what she just said. "I'll call you."

"OK. Let me know. One more thing, can you tell me anything?"

"Classified and we are under gag orders."

"This can only help you."

Derrick stands up and grabs her by the shoulders. "I know. I will handle this."

Alana caresses his face. "I love you."

He wraps his hands around her waist. "I know. I love you too. I *will* handle this."

Alana leaves his office and he watches her walk out the door with a smile on his face. Alana makes it to the elevator. She is in deep thought when John walks up to her.

He speaks in a coy English manner. "Hey there we meet again."

That was the worst impression she has ever heard. He doesn't even realize she just rolled her eyes. She smiles. She is trying to muster up the energy to have a conversation. John is quite handsome and she seems interested in him. Well not him. Sex. It's been a few days since she last spoke with Alex. She has to call him later to let off some steam.

"Why, hello. Again"

"You seem like you need a good cup of coffee. May I offer to purchase you one from one of my favorite places?"

"You know what? That would be quite lovely."

"So that means that I can drop the niceties?"

Alana laughs heartily. "Yes. So where is this place?"

"Oh, it's right around the corner."

"Where? Because I haven't seen a *good* coffee shop around here."

"OK. Follow me."

(He grabs her hand and she follows him around the corner to the cafeteria.)

Alana lets out a very haughty laugh. "Oh my God!" (Clears her throat.) "Well, I really wasn't expecting this." She points around the cafeteria. She thinks who in God's name decided it was a good idea to put a café on the 11th floor?

"Hey, don't judge a book by its cover. Just because it's the cafeteria – they have some good java."

"You know. As many times as I have been here – I never really paid attention to the cafeteria."

"Well, my dear, sometimes it just takes looking outside of the box."

"I thought it was "think outside of the box."

"Exactly. I changed it to fit me."

"When was this?"

"A long time ago. 1999 I think. I used to sit in a box all of my life."

She raises an eyebrow and chuckles. "Wow. I hope not a literal box."

"See, notta bad person am I?"

"I don't know that still remains to be seen."

He gasps and grabs at his heart. As if his English accent wasn't the worse. He began speaking in "Valley Girl". "OMG! Like. I totally can't believe you just said that."

They walk up to the counter. The clerk who has been staring at them since they walked in speaks up. "May I help you?"

John leans over the counter. Things could not be better for him at this moment. "Now come on Mel. Are you going to be that formal?"

Melissa is agitated. John is not the best of the best, but he flirts with her every day. "Well considering you have new company." She shoots a glance that only women can do.

John plays it off. "Oh this girl? I just thought I'd show her around and stuff. This is just Wells. I mean Alana. She is Derrick's sister."

"I see what you did there."

"Well I could have said; how do you say it? My future baby momma?"

(Melissa and Wells look at each other.)

In unison: "Uh, uh." They both laugh.

"Now how is that possible when I just had your baby two days ago?" Melissa says in a flirty voice.

"And you are back at work? Wow! That's some recovery."

"Well, I had to come back to work to keep him in line. Good thing too. What'll it be?"

"Well, the usual for me and you my lady?"

"I would like ... whatever he's having."

"Good Choice. Good choice. Make sure you make it just like I like."

Melissa glances at Alana as she walks over to the coffee machine. "You did make a good choice. You're going to get addicted like I did."

John laughs. "Yep. That's me. I am the coffee slinger."

(They all laugh. Melissa turns to make the coffee.)

"So that's pretty nice how close you and your brother are."

She hesitates. "Wait. What do you mean?"

"Well I can tell that you guys have a magical bond."

She is very leery. "Yeah we bonded when we were little."

"I never had that. I'm an only child. A miracle child."

"Really, why?"

"My mom was killed and they did an emergency C-section to save me. My dad was so heartbroken that he never remarried."

"If you don't mind me asking, what happened?"

"To this day, no one knows. All I know is that my mother is dead and my dad disappeared. So the speculation is he killed her then changed his identity. You know stuff that you see in the movies."

"Oh."

Melissa turns back around and hands them their coffee.

"Enjoy!"

"Will do. Thank you." He gives Melissa the exact change and places $2 in the tip jar. "Would you like to go for a walk?"

As they begin to walk away and before Alana has a chance to say no, he gives Melissa a farewell. "Bye Mel." He raises his eyebrows twice.

"See ya!"

They leave the building and walk toward the park.

John sniffs his coffee. "So what's the deal with you and Derrick? How come you two are so close?"

She takes a sip. "Our father was. Is. Real tough on us. So we just leaned on each other."

"Oh. Did he beat you?"

"Oh God no. He just had a way of making you feel – well – inadequate."

"I'm sorry. Let's talk happy thoughts."

"Happy thoughts?"

"Why yes. Like what gives you pleasure?"

"My pleasure in life is to travel and ice skate."

"Ice skate. I never would have pegged you as a skater."

"I looove to skate."

"May I have the pleasure of taking you skating tomorrow night?"

"Sure. I would like that."

"Then it's a date."

"A date? Hmmm. Ok. Yes!"

In the back of her mind she is thinking who said you can't have your cake and eat it too? Guys do it all the time and the release would be fabulous.

(Her phone rings. It's Alex. Speak of the devil.)

"Hello?"

"Hello my love."

"Alex! Hi!"

Her voice is a little too chipper for John's liking. He turns away from her to give her some privacy. Yet he can't help but think that there is more to this phone call. He stays by close enough to listen.

"I miss you already."

"I miss you too."

"Since you are no longer on the force. Can we now turn this into pure pleasure?"

"Maybe. So how's my favorite M.E.?"

"Things are going well. Listen, I need to talk to you about those cases. I know you don't work on the force any more but I need to pick your brain about something."

"Sure. That case is still open. When do you want to meet?"

"As soon as possible."

"I'm on my way." (Turning to John.) "I'm sorry."

"That's completely understandable. It's just tomorrow – you have to turn your phone off. Deal?"

"Deal." (Smiles.)

Derrick is at the Local Grocery Mart not far from his house. The night has turned eerie and cold. Derrick has a long sad face and anyone looking at him can tell that his heart is heavy. He is purchasing the usual items that he would have normally purchased for Terry. The clerks look sympathetic and curious. Hannah quietly clears her throat.

Clerks Need Love Too

"Um, hi Derrick. How are you doing?"

"I'm okay considering. You know."

"So, why..."

(Derrick shoots her a look.)

"Oh. Well if you need someone to talk to. I'm here." As she said it even though it was quite sincere, she knew that it sounded very desperate. Derrick perks up a bit which makes her feel a bit relieved.

"You know, I think I can take you up on that. You have always been a beautiful person (caresses her face), but, for tonight, I need this time alone." (He opens his wallet and pulls out a card with cash. He hands it to Hannah.) "Besides, I promised you if there was an opening, you would be first candidate, right?" (He laughs and then leans over and kisses her on the cheek.)

Hannah Chuckles. "Wow."

(The other clerk looks in amazement and smiles.)

"Yeah, wow. I will need someone you know. Terry's gone and my sister is leaving me."

"What do you mean? This now kind of feels like a rebound."

"Ms. Wells has decided to move to Cape Verde. However, I have a lot going on here that I just can't leave behind. Besides you can't be a rebound unless you feel like a rebound."

"Cape Verde? Really? Why so far?"

"Let's just say that things are getting tough for her."

"But she never backs down from a fight."

"Well, (He shrugs his shoulders.) I guess this time she is."

"Hmmm."

"Here is my number." (He picks up the pen on the counter. He takes her hand and writes his number down.) "Call me in the morning. I would like to take you to breakfast."

"Absolutely." She looks at her hand and smiles.

Derrick walks out and looks back for one last glance. Hannah stares at the door longingly before turning to the other clerk and squealing like school girls. Hannah's long blonde hair sways as she sways in the moment. The more she thinks about the future breakfast date the more beet red her face becomes. Her crystal blue eyes sparkles like the sweetest sapphire.

Derrick makes it home. It's the same look. Nothing has changed since Terry's death. He is sitting in the exact spot where he and Terry last made love in front of the fire place. He's holding Terry's favorite pillow. In the background it begins to rain. There is thunder and lightning as the rain begins to pour Derrick begins crying uncontrollably.

It is a new day. The sun is shining brightly through the blinds and he has not moved. He has fallen asleep in the same spot. The candles have burned themselves out. The phone rings.

Derrick reaches over and looks at the phone. It's Hannah. His voice is sleepy and hoarse from crying all night. "Hello."

He yawns and stretches.

"Good morning Derrick this is your wake up call. Sounds like you need about two cups of coffee." She sounds overly excited.

He smiles. "Good morning. Make that three."

Hannah chuckles. "Well, I know of a place where you can get good food and coffee."

"Well that's great because, I need both."

"OK well shower and shave and call me back and I'll tell you where to meet me."

"Will do."

"Then it's a date." She hangs up.

As he watches the call disconnect he becomes aroused.

"That it is Hannah. That it is."

He gets up and heads to the shower to get ready.

Time to Go

That same morning. Alana is in her apartment. There are many boxes scattered throughout the living room as she's preparing to leave. She's packing and looking at pictures. She has a sad but happy look on her face. The doorbell rings. She stands up to answer the door. She looks out the peephole. She is wearing short shorts and a tank top. She glances over at the full length mirror. She knows she's hot. She opens the door so that John gets a full view right away.

John is startled. "Hi."

"John! Hi."

"I thought I'd come by and take you to breakfast. Well, actually bring you breakfast." He lifts the bag from McDonald's.

"Oh." She grasps her heart. "How sweet." The aroma reminds Alana that she hasn't eaten since she woke up at three this morning.

"May I come in?"

"Where are my manners? Of course, please come in."

"I brought a variety of stuff. I didn't know what you like so."

"I'm not picky. I can eat just about anything."

"Interesting. I do, however, know what you like in your coffee." With a devilish grin, he reaches out to hand her the coffee.

"Yeah? What if I said I didn't want any?"

"Then I would be in big trouble. I brought you a large."

"Wow, you went all out? You big spender you."

"I'm trying."

"I know. You get an E for Effort."

"Is that even a letter grade?"

"Yep. It's in the new handbook." She smirks and takes the coffee. "Mmmm. Now that's good."

"I have come to realize that you have to be careful of which place to go to. It's seems that each one has their own style of making things. So, I have my favorites of where I go."

"Make sure you give me that list because this is great!"

"Will do. So dig in."

"You don't have to tell me twice." She is inhaling the food and making noises. John is amazed.

"Ah!"

Alana shoots him a quizzical look. "What was that for?"

"I have NEVER seen a woman who was not afraid to eat in front of me on the first date."

She speaks with a mouth full of food. "This is a date?"

"We're out, there's food, yep, looks like a date to me."

"That's fascinating since *I'm* home and *you* are out. I thought our date would be tonight as planned when we go ice skating."

"Nah. I thought I'd change it up a little. I couldn't wait to see you."

"I know. I was a little anxious to see you too. Secretly, I was hoping that you would call or something. Truthfully, it's been a while since I've had company other than my brother.

"I plan on changing that."

"Really? And what are your plans sir?"

"I thought I would start with this." (He kisses her. He can't tell if it's the syrup, jelly or her lips that are just plain sweet.) "And move on to other things." (He kisses her again this time it's a little more passionate and she doesn't resist.)

Things get a little more heated and she leads him to the bedroom. They are completely into it. She slams him against the wall with the force of 10 cops while kissing him. He does not wince. It turns him on. Assuming that this is the norm for her, he takes her by the arms and swings her around and grabs her by the neck. "Not bad for a nerd." She thinks as he thrusts his pelvis into hers. They are rocking back and forth and with each thrust she feels how hard as a brick he is.

He pulls off her shirt and grabs a breast in both hands. She is now happy she was not wearing a bra. Because her curiosity is piqued – she quickly thrusts her hands down his pants. He groans in excitement and she feels it move. She unbuckles his pants and slowly slides down the wall kissing his abdomen getting on her knees. The phone rings and by the ringtone she knows it is Derrick.

"Wait. I have to get that." She stands up and makes it just in time to answer the last ring. At the same time she is leading John to the bed. She pushes him down. He sits there. She is standing in between his legs and he is kissing her all over and caressing her nipples. The volume is loud enough to hear the conversation.

She exhales loudly. "Hello?"

"Hey baby – how are you?"

John is still kissing all over her and she's into every kiss and touch. He slides 2 fingers under her shorts. Her legs buckle. She stutters. "I'm, I'm good. What's going on?"

"I thought I'd call and see how you were. Why do you sound out of...Oh my God who is it?"

"What are you talking about?"

She steps away.

"I know that heavy breathing and stuttering. All your work out equipment is packed. I know because I'm the one who broke it down and packed it for you."

"There are videos and shows – you know."

"Yeah, but your breathing is different."

She is wanting to rush him off the phone because her body is burning hot and her blood is boiling. "It's nothing. Anything else?"

"Yeah there is. When John is done, please ask him if he could be at the lab at 3 so we can have a meeting and go over some stuff for Monday."

"What?!"

"I'm outside…" He Laughs. "I was coming to see you but I see you are a little bit busy. It's about time. I hope it's good. Must be nice that someone else has your time."

"Come on, you know it could never be like that. You are always the number one man in my life."

"Love you."

"Love you more. Well. I have plans too so – bye. Before she could ask with who he hangs up.

Derrick looks at John's car. It is a blue Chevy Camaro. "Interesting."

Alana looks at her phone as it disconnects. "Ha!"

"Wow. That's a little creepy."

"Nah. That's just brotherly love."

"I thought we agreed that your phone would be off."

"Yeah but that arrangement wasn't until later tonight. *This* was an unexpected but welcomed visit." (She begins kissing him again.)

"May I finish what we started my Queen?"

"I'd be disappointed if you didn't."

They continue to make love and all is blissful. She begins fantasizing about Alex. Her mind races from Alex to John until they collide and what she wants more than anything is to be in bed with both of them at the same time right now. The fantasy becomes so hard and fast that when John gives a full thrust against her – she climaxes and screams so loud that it makes him jump. He follows suit and together they reach the peak of it all.

He collapses and immediately she stands up to go shower. He turns in a bewildered moment. She walks away as if nothing just happened. Her naked body in full view, she walks over to the TV stand to turn on the news. There is much clamor in the background and she glances to see her father. She stops dead in her tracks.

He is standing outside of the Channel 4 News Station. Teresa Bills' body is lying in plain view. It is lifeless. Police are gathered around canvassing the area and speaking to witnesses.

Handled

Adam is very angry that this is not being handled correctly.

At this point, Alana is not sure if she has gotten more pleasure from the chaos on television involving her father or what just happened between her and John.

The anger in Adam's voice is apparent. "Get these people out of here. If you haven't noticed this is a crime scene."

An officer standing by is startled by his voice and jumps into action. "Yes sir."

Chief Williams walks up and pulls him aside out of earshot of the cameras. "Adam you gotta get a hold of this and quick. This is getting out of hand. At first we thought this was some sort of connection but now it's too random. What is the deal?"

"I don't know. What I do know is that my daughter was possibly onto something and you my friend let her go. If I know her like I hope I do she'll be back."

"But when? By that time it will be too late."

"Never underestimate the power of a woman. She'll be back."

Finley lazily walks over to join the conversation.

He speaks with confidence of his friend and confidant. "Of course she will. At least for my sake. I can't handle this like she does."

Chief Williams glances his way. "I have to admit she was one of the best. So what do you know?"

Finley shrugs his shoulders. "Same old thing – different body."

"Get it over to the M.E."

"10-4. Sir." He walks off.

Chief Williams turn back to Adam. "Adam man, this is seriously crazy. We are up to six unsolved murder cases. It won't be long before the President of the United States is involved."

"Hmmph. It ain't that serious, but we do need to find out what's going on. I'll call her and see if I can meet with her."

"Yeah. You do that."

From off to side, another officer is scouring through evidence. He gets very excited. The only problem is – he tells the whole world.

"Chief I think we got something!" He screams so loud that the news cameras turn. They begin running to where he is. In return, several officers block them and tell them to step back. They are disgusted that he could have made such a rookie move.

The Chief and Adam walk over smoothly and coolly to the officer.

Williams furrows his brow in anger, "What?"

"It's another note."

Adam slips on a pair of gloves and takes the note to examine it. He begins to read it aloud in a voice barely above a whisper so as to not tip off anyone else around. **They** are watching.

"Now you are getting as good as her if you found this note, but you're still too slow. By the time you finish reading this two more will be dead. How long will it take before you bring the killer, i.e. me to justice? This is too fun and too hilarious to not keep going. It's a shame that we lost a valuable player, but one has stepped up to take the spot. Let's see if he really is as good as they say he is. I personally like a challenge."

Chief Williams throws up his hands. "Hold on. What does that mean?"

Adam has this discerned look on his face. "**They** know *us.*"

Finally, Some Answers

Questions Answered

It's 3pm. The news reporter's body in full view. Her body is stunning. Alex contemplates if necrophilia is really such a bad thing. He gets his answer when in walks Alana.

"Well, well, well. Aren't you a sight for sore eyes?"

"Judging from your eyes and that body over there. I don't think yours are quite that sore. Besides, it hasn't been that long."

"Long enough. So, I'll get right to it. First things first. I was baffled by the question you asked me a few weeks ago. So I did what all curious people do. I looked up that Darmstadtium. If I'm even saying it right. It is on the latest periodic table. Darmstadtium is a radioactive, synthetic element about which little is known. It is classified as a metal and is expected to be a solid at room temperature. It has no real form and just as soon as you see it – it's gone. It's highly radioactive but has a life span of maybe a few seconds. It's still in the works. Way back in the day, not much had been known, but scientists have made strides. It's in between a metal and a gas. I did some checking and called a buddy of mine and he said that there is testing for a new chemical, mind and body thing, that is or was top secret and there's only one place that's producing it at this time."

Alana is sick to her stomach. The words taste like acid as she speaks them, "Lingerman Technologies."

"Right. Wait. How'd you know?"

"I guess I forgot to tell you my brother works there. That explains D.O.D and NSA."

"What?"

"I went to see my brother a few days ago and it was crazy bananas. While everyone else was all in a panic – he was calm like a sunny, breezy day."

"I see. And you saw this Darmstadtium..."

"At his house on some papers."

"That doesn't mean anything though. A lot of people have access to this not just him."

"This is what I pray, but no one is as smart as he is there."

"I see. Anyway, moving on. I also noticed and got to thinking what if this is just a test run. Randomly selecting people in age, race, status and things of that nature. So, I looked at brain wave patterns."

"How when they are dead?"

"I took a shot in the dark. I scanned the brain to get any last activity or see what it looks like after the fact. Shockingly there is a pattern."

"What kind of pattern?"

"From the activity or lack thereof – these people died like they were murdered."

"News flash – they were."

"Not in that sense. You know, actually MURDERED. Like if I came over right now and strangled you with that belt."

"I'd like to see you try."

There was something in that statement that gave Alex a serious chill. He was looking for the sexy flirting and it was not there. This was something else.

"Let me explain. The news reporter. Very healthy young woman and pretty to boot. She has the brain activity of someone being smothered. Affixation. However, there are no markings or signs of struggle, but it's what her brain indicates right? Like her brain told her she was dying so – she died. This homeless person. With him, it looks like he was poisoned right? Like an overdose of some kind. The lividity of his body. The way his hands are. It's strange. But, here's the deal. I order tox screens on everybody and low and behold. Nothing. I honestly think somehow the two are linked and what needs to happen at this point is you need to go back – at least to solve these cases. If this Darmstadtium is as powerful as they say it is. It's not going to stop no time soon. I took and kept samples of all of the bodies from before."

"I'm not going back but I will pass it on."

"They need you. NOT your father."

"I know. I'm going to meet with Finley later. Just so you know I leave for Cape Verde in two days."

"What?"

"I'm leaving and more than likely I won't be coming back."

"How's that possible? I thought I was going to get a chance now. I mean the chemistry of it all? Now you are leaving? Couldn't you have said something BEFORE we became intimate?"

"That's quite feminine. Please don't make me regret sleeping with you. Besides - I just can't stay here. I need to get out. Away from here. I need a change of scenery. Plus that's been my dream."

"How come so soon?"

"Given everything that is happening? I so don't want to be around when the shit hits the fan."

"What do you mean? What are you thinking?"

Alana looks down at her watch and realizes that she's about to be late. "I'm thinking I gotta go. I'll relay the information on to the proper authorities."

"Talk to you later?"

"Yeah. Sure. Whatever."

She waves a hand back at him. He can't tell whether it was a goodbye or her being dismissive. Alex stands back and stares at her. He knows that she knows something.

All Fingers Point to Derrick

Derrick is holding a team meeting. Everyone's face is flushed and it's as though they are afraid to speak. Derrick looks very serious. No one bats an eye as he speaks. John rushes in a little disheveled.

Derrick makes light of it as he walks up to the team considering what he knew from this morning. "John – so nice of you to join us."

John scratches his head, "Uh yeah. I was a little tied up."

Derrick shoots him a glance and a smile. "I bet." (He turns back to the group.) "As I was saying, things are really thick around here and the investigation is well underway. Whoever leaked the data will be prosecuted and I'm so hoping that none of my team is involved in this. We know for a fact that T.J. was involved. And this is why he may have met an unfortunate demise. This is not good for anyone involved. The authorities will be here asking questions soon. Mr. Lingerman can only hold them off for so long. You will be fingerprinted, probably go through a lie detector test and questioned. My advice to you is to cooperate fully and whomever is involved make it easy for yourself and all of us."

John clears his throat nervously, "This is terrible."

Derrick looks at him very solemnly, "I know."

"Well, I tell you one thing. You have my full cooperation."

At that everyone nods in agreement.

"I mean, seriously guys – they are pulling tapes. Watching and detecting your every move. If just one thing looks out of place - that's it. That's your family, your career and worst of all the end of me as I'm your TL. Don't do this to us. You'll ruin the company. Maybe you don't care, but we do. I have never pleaded before in my life except for one time and now I'm at this crossroads again."

A second tech steps up. She is a middle aged, skinny woman. Her voice is shaky. "Look, he's right. I have a family to look after and my husband is not recovering as fast as or as well as we all hoped for. I'm quite sure that this could be swept under the carpet and prosecution will be lenient. Just come forward. The longer it lingers the worse it will be."

Another tech steps forward a portly, balding man. "OK. This is what I know. Maybe we are looking in the wrong direction. T.J. was always around asking questions. Maybe there's some way to pull his phone records or whatever and see who he's been talking to?"

Derrick looks up with explosion in his eyes and stares directly at him, "Are you sure?"

The tech nods like a toddler. "Yes. He's been selling our ideas and taking a few as his own for months."

"Why haven't you come forward until now?"

He shrugs his shoulders. "Honestly, I didn't care because I have a job offer somewhere else and knew that all the new stuff I have would land me a better position."

"Wow. You are just a plethora of information now."

"I have to be truthful. This didn't bother me until now. When I realized it may jeopardize any job that I have.

"Selfish much?"

A fourth tech, Linda speaks up. "I don't know anything. I only know what Max told me."

Derrick voice raises to a level no one has heard before. This takes everyone by surprise. "And you all held this from me? I have been there for all of you and this is what I get?"

Max turns to face him directly, "Let's not go crazy. As you are the TL AND he was your best friend – suspicious much?"

Derrick goes to respond until he realizes Max is right, he calms down. "This does look really bad for me huh?"

John feels that he now has "in-law" status. He steps up to pat Derrick on the back. "It's just bad for all of us. This thing has gone way too far." (He turns to the team.) "But you guys really should have come forward a long time ago. Maybe we could have gotten a handle on this beforehand."

Max speaks in a disgusted tone. "Look the bottom line is you do what you must. I will be cooperative, but I don't have much info except for what I gave you."

Derrick loses all of his energy. "I guess that's all I can ask for. I know this is stressful. I personally have a lot to deal with on my own, but we need to also get our acts together to prove to the D.O.D. that top secret info is just that – top secret. Life does go on and we can get through this. Our numbers have been looking great and let's keep up the good work. I believe in you guys so let's do what we can to end this and move on."

John tries to make light of the situation. "I'm with you on this. I'm just surprised Channel 2 didn't know what was going on."

Tech 2 turns abruptly. "Hey! Watch it."

"You are the town gossip." (Everyone chuckles in agreement.) "Besides it's all in good humor."

Derrick regroups. "Anyway, let's pull this last project together to get the final numbers for Mr. L. If we can get an "attaboy" – then he may forgive us for this."

(Everyone turns to leave to their designated stations. Derrick pulls John aside.)

John hesitates before he speaks. "Hey look man – I'm so sorry. I know this is the anniversary and all. I didn't mean to pull your sister away."

"No that's cool. I'm just wondering how you were able to lure her so quickly."

John puffs out his chest like he's the alpha male. "Good looks and charm."

"More like good luck."

(They both laugh.)

"Seriously though Derrick. If you want to bail out of here and put your mind somewhere else, I will head this up for you."

"No, I think I'll stick around for a while just to be sure things are going smoothly and he doesn't need anything."

"True. You know it has to be big when you get him in here on a Saturday."

"You telling me."

"What do think?"

"Right now, I don't know what to think."

"I hope all goes well."

"Hope? We need more like prayer to survive this. Other than that, you know my sister is leaving in a couple of days?"

"That explains the boxes."

"Yeah so I don't know how far you are planning on taking this."

"Long distance relationships can work. You just have to know how."

"Just how *far* do you think she's going?"

"I am sure it's not too far. I know she loves you guys. So I am "guessing a few states over? Not too far?"

"No. Try another country."

"Wait. What?"

"She's moving to Africa."

"Get out."

"I might."

"Seriously?"

"This is well beyond my control. Yeah (scoffs), the heat will be on me and she really wants me to come with."

"Oh. You didn't mention that."

"I really hadn't considered it until Tess just pointed out that I look just as suspicious. And all fingers could point back to me. I mean seriously. I am the team lead and I have just as much access, if not more to everything as T.J. did."

"Ah. (John is barely audible. Derrick leans in to hear him.) How far *is* your involvement?"

"I have absolutely NO involvement. But still. I had suspicions but I couldn't put my finger on it."

"Does The Boss know?"

"I'm not sure. I can't tell if he's different because of this, losing his wife or what."

"Well. Let's get to work before we don't have a job prematurely."

"Right."

Derrick pats John on the back and leaves. He heads to his office. He sits down and stares at Alana's picture on the desk. He softly caresses the frame.

"Baby girl. What are we into?"

The day passes by. Day fades to night. Alana is sitting on the floor in her apartment. She is going through her things preparing to go ice skating.

She finds herself humming a song she used to hear her mom sing all the time. She knows the song, but can't place her finger on it. She just remembers her mom singing it when things were going really well with her marriage. She remembers how bright her mom's face was when she very much in love.

"Wow, I guess I haven't been this happy in a very long time."(She chuckles. Her phone rings. Her heart drops and butterflies form in her stomach. Not looking at the caller id she answers the phone.) "Hello?"

(Well 1 out of 3 ain't bad.)

Derrick's deep and sultry voice rings through. "Hey baby."

"Hey!"

"Getting ready for your... date?"

"Of course. We're going ice skating."

"Hmmm. You haven't been ice skating in a very long time."

"I know. It's wild. I mean really wild."

"I'm glad to see one of us is happy."

"Jealous?"

"Never that."

"Well, how is it going with uh Hannah?"

Derrick pauses thinking about how Hannah does not compare to Alana, "Pretty good I guess."

"Why don't you guys come along with? I mean you were supposed to meet her for coffee. This may be a good way to make it up to her."

"Not a bad idea. I guess. Let me call her and I'll call you back."

"K."

Derrick hangs up to call Hannah. He gets her voicemail. Reluctantly he is happy that she did not answer. Then he hears her voice. All she says is "leave a message" and thought it was the sweetest message ever. Maybe he should give her a chance.

"Hey Hannah it's me Derrick. I am wondering if you would like to go ice skating with me and my sister Alana. I'm sorry for not getting back with you, but I figure this would be a good way to make it up *and* meet my sister. Give me a call when you get this message."

It's a Date

Alana is putting the finishing touches on her hair and outfit when the doorbell rings. She runs to the door very excitedly. She looks out the peep hole and sees a dozen red roses.

(She gasps.) "Oh my. He's pulling out all the stops." (She opens the door wide. She reaches for the flowers.) "You shouldn't have."

"But I had to. I feel something for you Alana. It's like you have a part of my heart and soul. What did you do to me?" (He wraps his arms around her and pulls her close.)

"I don't know. I was kinda gonna ask you the same thing."

"I guess it's an unspoken attraction – you know?"

"Yeah I guess so."

(He snuggles into her neck.) "I was thinking that since we have some time… why don't we…" (He whispers into her ear.)

(Her eyes widen with excitement. She turns and runs toward the room.) "If you can catch me first!"

"I'll even give you a head start!"

Alana screams and runs faster towards the door. John looks at her and smiles. He quickly catches her and they fall into the bed. He caresses her on the face. Then he licks her lips slowly with his tongue.

"God Alana. You are so beautiful. I need you in my life. It's like you've opened up a brand new side of me."

"You know? I feel the same way."

"What's funny is how you never really paid any attention to me before now."

"I guess I was just focused on my job and stuff. Derrick was the only man in my life besides my father and I guess I thought that was all that I needed."

"Interesting. Go on."

"Go on?"

"Yes. Please explain to me why you felt that way."

"My, um, husband used to beat me."

"Now, I find THAT hard to believe."

"It's true. All the time. I wasn't married long. We met while I was in college. Sometimes he even used mental abuse too. My dad warned me about him but I was in love or so I thought. My dad could never prove it because I knew how to hide it. I mean, really well. So after all of that. I guess I just felt all I needed was my career, brother and dad."

"How did you escape?"

"As I got older. I got smarter. I told him flat out one day that he could die and no one would know. He knew that I have a chemistry background plus I was becoming an officer. My dad was already popular and this is Derrick's specialty. So one day, he decided to test me. So I proved to him that it was a promise and not a threat. Derrick and I made him very sick for a month. He flat lined twice. I was secretly hoping he would die, but then that would be homicide and neither of us wanted that."

(John sits up a little nervously.) "How long ago was that?"

"It's going on about 5 or 6 years now."

"Oh." A sour look comes across his face. Could Derrick be lying to him? Is she lying right now? Is this even real what he's hearing?

"Don't look like that. I had to get out."

"Why didn't you just leave?"

"I tried, but it was hard trying to leave and keep it from my father at the same time. Plus, my ex tried to kill me three times. He would be missing today if my family knew half of the story I'm telling you now. Derrick also helped in protecting me. So I really had no worries."

"I just can't. I just can't believe it."

"Neither can I. With as much training that I've had. I've arrested people for less and yet I was going through it. It's really amazing. In a bad way."

"So what happened?"

"I sat him down when he was having his revelation moment and I sternly asked him if he wanted to get better and live. He looked at me with this strange look on face as if he had come to an epiphany. I looked at him and just laughed. I mean I laughed so hard! I laughed so hard knowing it was me doing all of this to him that it gave me chills. It echoed through the air. Then suddenly I stopped and stared him dead in his eyes and said 'you know it was me now don't you'."

"Um."

"He swallowed hard and begged me to stop. He was all like. (She begins whining.) 'Make it stop. Please God, make it stop'. I told him to sign the divorce papers and disappear out of my life for good. He moved to another state and has not attempted to contact me. I mean it was so easy and he didn't see it coming! How cool is that?"

She laughs that same menacing laugh and it sends chills down his back. The crazy part is he doesn't know whether to bolt for the door or rip her clothes off. It was actually kind of sexy – this whole other side of her.

"I don't know. You scare me." (He laughs nervously.) "Remind me to stay on your good side."

"My good side ay?" (She straddles him.) "Well let's start with some kissing and see what happens from there."

"Kissing is my specialty."

"Hmm. I so happen to like your kisses too.

"Really?"

"Yep!"

John pulls her in close and begins to kiss her passionately and unbutton her blouse. It gets really heavy. Her hairs falls onto her shoulders. The phone rings. He continues trying to ignore the phone. He recognizes the ring tone.

"Don't get that."

"But it's my brother."

"I know. Can't he wait?"

She glances at him. "What 5 minutes?"

"Harsh." (He grabs her hand to prevent her from answering.) "No. However long it takes."

"I guess I could let it go to voicemail."

"That's my girl. You'll have plenty of other times to chat with bro. Now's my time and I want to show you how much I love you."

As much as that statement sounded so good. It made her sick to her stomach. She really enjoys spending what little time she has with John and she still yearns for Alex. She makes a mental note to call him later. For now she is going to enjoy this moment.

"Please do."

Time passes. They are lying in bed talking more.

"Wow." She chuckles.

"Every day is different and every day is better, stronger."

"I know. It's like you put a curse or chemical spell on me or something. It's some unforeseen bond. You know?"

"Yeah. I do."

"Caaaarrrreful, with those words."

"You know. It could be a possibility." (He leans over the bed and grabs his pants and pulls out a small box. He comes back up to her and pulls her close.) "I've been thinking about this since the day I saw you at the elevators."

"Really? What about?"

"About us and how you make me feel."

"She has a slightly puzzled look. Her heart is racing. She begins panting. "So what are you saying?"

"What I'm saying is... That I love you. I could see myself with you for the rest of my life. I mean everything in my life and about me with you. You have stolen my heart like no woman has ever done. Quicker than what I could have imagined. Alana (He turns her to fully face him.) will you be my wife?" (He opens up the box and the ring is exquisite with diamonds and sapphires. This is no ordinary ring. It is very expensive. So ornate. How could he have gotten a ring so quickly? More importantly, why?)

(Alana gasps and holds her heart. Her mouth is open, but nothing comes out.)

"Well, say *something*."

"John, it's beautiful. How did you know I like sapphires?"

"I know your birthday is in September so I took a stab at it. But you kinda have to say something or I will feel foolish."

(She begins to speak when the phone rings again. It's Derrick. Thank God.) "I have to get it this time. I invited him with us if that is ok? So he's probably calling back to say yay or nay."

John sighs. "Go ahead."

She reaches over him to get the phone. He makes no attempt to touch her.

"Hello?"

"Where are you?"

"At home why?"

"Did you forget about skating?"

"I was kinda in the middle of something."

"Or more like something was in the middle of you." (He laughs and John hears it through the phone.) "We've been here for about 20 minutes or so. Are you coming because normally you are never late?"

"Oh my God! I didn't know it was that late." (She glances over by the clock.) "OK we're on our way." (She hangs up before he can respond.)

Derrick looks at the phone and shakes his head.

"Well, is she coming?"

(He chuckles to himself.) "More than you know."

"Great! I'm pretty excited to see the other woman in your life."

"Me too. Me too."

Alana jumps out the bed to go get freshened up. John pulls her back down to finish the conversation.

"They are there waiting on us."

"And I'm waiting on you."

(Surprised.) "Oh. Look. I know what we have is strong but I don't know what to do or say. I leave Monday."

"That's why I thought if I asked you today you wouldn't leave. I need you more than you know. I can't live my life without you."

"I know for a fact that you can. But. John… I… I have to do this."

"No you don't. Whatever you lose I can replace. Alana you are my heart."

"You know the situation right now."

"I don't give a rat's ass. All I know is that since being with you – I feel different."

"I have to talk to my brother. Can you give me that? Until tonight or tomorrow?"

"Yes. I just need you right now. But let's get dressed since we have guests waiting."

"Alright."

They quickly get freshened up and leave. They are walking to John's car and all she could think about was Alex. She knew well that her heart was being pulled in three different directions. She has on the ring and she is holding John's hand while they drive. The song "Because You Love Me" plays in the background. Alana is at peace and takes in the moment. She is glowing.

They finally arrive at the skating rink. Derrick and Hannah are sharing a drink. Just as Derrick looks up, John & Alana are walking in. He holds the door open for her. Derrick instantly senses that something is off. He smiles any way.

Hannah whispers in his ear, "By the look on your face. I take it that that's your sister?"

"Yep."

"Besides she looks just like you."

"Oh really." He raises an eyebrow and tilts his head.

"Oh I didn't mean like that. I. I."

Alana and John walk over to the table. Derrick stands up and hugs her and shakes John's hand.

"So glad to see that you can make it."

"We were a little busy."

"What is that on your finger?"

"We need to talk."

Derrick turns to Hannah. "Give us a minute?"

Hannah and John speaks simultaneously, "Sure."

(Derrick and Alana walk away.)

"He loves his sister. I didn't even notice the ring."
Hannah has a bit of uneasiness in her voice.

"Well, Derrick is like that. He has a very keen sense for things especially when it comes to her."

"Sometimes some siblings have such a strong bond that *nothing* can separate them."

"Hmph."

(Alana and Derrick move out of earshot from Hannah and John. He moves in close to her.)

"What are you doing? He didn't waste any time huh?"

"No, I guess he did not. What do you think?"

"This is crazy, but how do you feel?"

"Derrick... I... I think I could love him."

"Whoa."

"I know. But you know that..."

"I know. I have decided to go with you."

(Excitedly.) "This is great! I knew I paid for that extra ticket for a reason. I'm glad they don't have extradition either."

"Wait. You really..."

(He's interrupted by Hannah and John.)

John attempts to speak in the most alpha male tone. "OK times up. Besides whatever it is it can wait. We are here to enjoy ourselves." (He smiles.) "Right?"

Alana likes the way he tried to take charge. "Right. Let's go."

The rest of the night goes smoothly and the hours spent at the rink only feels like minutes. They say their good-byes and Alana and John head back to her place. They are sitting on the couch. The television is on just for background noise and they are snuggled in each other's arms.

"You really know how to woo a girl."

"Women are my specialty. Specifically you. I have longed for you since the first day I saw you."

"Really? That would be years."

"Yeah I know."

"I mean a lot of years."

"Um hmm." (He begins lightly kissing her.)

"So. What did you do while you longed for me? Obviously you never married and I never heard of or saw a girlfriend."

"You were also oblivious because you had your own life to deal with, but you know I didn't know you like I do now. I never got a chance to get close enough to you. Actually, you kinda intimidated me."

"Me? Really?"

(Through kisses.) "Um hmm. Yep. That's about it."

Alana scoffs and laughs. "Seriously?"

"Yeah."

"OK so what did you do to uh cope?"

(He leans over and whispers in her ear. Her eyes widen and her mouth drops open.) "Satisfied?"

She clears her throat. "Uh wow yeah. I guess sometimes you should know when to stop asking questions!"

(John grabs her and pulls her under the covers. He adjusts the length of his body to fit them both on the couch.)

"John, it's so weird that I feel so safe and warm when I am next to you."

"So do I get an answer today or tomorrow or never?"

"One of those."

"So. Am I to also fear your father? Or can I get in good with your mom and all is blissful?"

"Truthfully, my mom is even harder than my dad even though he's a prick."

"Huh. Most girls don't refer to their fathers like that."

"You don't really know my father."

"I would if you tell me."

"OK. You know with everything in the news. That was my investigation."

"I know. I saw you on the TV. Plus when you spoke with your brother."

"So, my Chief jumps my ass and I'm already stressed out."

"And? What does this have to do with your father?"

"It gets worse when my dad gets involved. I mean – he came in and had to show that he was the man or whatever. I did the majority of the leg work and he gets the glory."

"Is that why you quit?"

"Not only that, but he makes me feel like I'm worthless and I let him down."

"How can someone make you feel that way when you are as strong as you are? Look at what you have endured."

"You just have no idea. We had to be strong. No child of his was going to be a slacker."

"I see so much bitterness in that."

"Well. Even though I'm clearly his favorite because I followed in his footsteps, he basically read me my rights and told me to get it together because my actions had an effect on everyone that I'm involved with. So feeling worthless, I went home and drank myself to sleep because he made me feel like I was 15 again and I cried right in front of him. I guess I kinda did feel like I let him down. This was supposed to be my moment to shine and I blew it under pressure."

"That's because it wasn't your pressure to begin with. I see everyone relies on you and no one should feel like they have to save the world. You can only do what's within your power. And for what it's worth – I know you can come back from all of this."

"And it is stuff like that that makes me want to fall in love with you."

"Well good. I've done my job. Since that's the past, let's keep it there. Let's focus on the future."

"It no longer looks gray and empty."

"That's what I like to hear. I really do love you."

Derrick and Hannah

Derrick is sitting at his desk in the bedroom. He is going over documents. On his computer, he has multiple files open. He glances over at Hannah who begins to stir. The evening went very well for the two of them. They decided to stay at his place.

Hannah sits ups in the bed and stretches. "Mmmm. Good morning."

"Good morning."

"You were restless for a while."

"I know. I'm sorry. My mind was racing and I couldn't sleep."

"After all of that. You couldn't sleep?"

"I know. I should still be asleep." He gives a wide smile.

"Well, I for one had a wonderful sleep."

"I know. I left you and went for a walk and you were still asleep."

"Honestly?"

"Yes. I could have killed you in your sleep and you wouldn't have even known it."

"Wow! I guess so. I normally don't sleep that heavy especially in a new place."

"Well hopefully, this will be your home soon too right?"

"I hope so."

"It makes no sense to wait. We both know what we want."

"If that's the case. We can start tomorrow."

"Actually, there's one hitch."

"Let me guess. Your sister?"

"Sort of."

"What is it?"

"You've seen in the news about what's going on with the murders?"

"Yeah and?"

"That was her case. Until my father took over. Things are really heating up and we think it's best if we leave."

"We meaning you and her? What's the deal between you two?"

"We've been through more than the average siblings and we just have each other's back that's all."

"Truthfully, it's seems a little more than that. So what do you want?"

"I want you. I need you in my life. Terry's gone and you have filled a big void in my life. I have known you for a very long time and secretly – I have contemplated being with you."

"You're treating me like rebound?! Really??"

"NO! I love you. I love every moment with you so far. I'm just asking for you to come with us. She should be asking John the same question right about now."

"I guess you two are inseparable."

Derrick gets up and crawls back in bed behind her and holds her close.

"And neither will be you and I if you just say yes. A new country and a new life. You won't have to worry or care about a thing. Throw caution to the wind and just be with me."

"You want me to leave everything and everyone behind?"

"So am I. I was hesitant at first as well. Frankly, I would love to be able to get from under my father's thumb and just live without living to his standards."

"Derrick. I don't know."

"You are a cashier at a local grocery store. What do you have to lose? Just do it."

"I'll have to think about. I can't say that it's love. But I can say I did want to be with you and I still do, but this is a bit more than I could imagine."

He caresses her inner thigh and nibbles on her ear. Her body shifts and moves to the rhythm of every stroke. Each hand movement gets closer to her already hungering desires.

Derrick whispers in her ear. "Just don't think about it and just do it. If you want to be with me this is what we have to do."

"Please."

"Are you begging for more?"

"Yes."

"Then say it."

"Please don't stop. I want more."

"Good girl. Then you will come with me?"

"More than you know."

"Fine." He thrusts three fingers inside of her and she screams not in pain, but in pure pleasure. Derrick knows he has her now.

"And what I ask of you?"

She is barely audible from breathing so heavily. "Give me some time to think about it."

"Time is of the essence and I don't have a lot of it."

Hannah turns around to face him. She grabs his fully erect penis and thrusts it in her mouth. He grabs her hair and wraps it in his hand. He thrusts his hips forward as she bobs her head. Never before had he felt such warm lips and gained such pleasure over controlling someone including Terry. He jerks and Hannah realizes that it is only a matter of time. She quickly positions him inside of her and she rides him hard. They both begin to moan and sweat before climaxing so hard that they move the bed.

They slumped down on the bed. Derrick fluffs out the pillows. As he lay down, Hannah rests her head on his chest. He strokes her hair. He's thinking that the least he could do is be honest to her.

"It's only a matter of time before they come after me."

"Why would they come after you?"

"They need a suspect. Someone has to go to jail right?"

"But why you?"

"Because, my dear, there is more to the story than you'll ever find out.

"Seriously. What *is* your involvement?"

"I knew T.J. was up to no good. I knew he sold proprietary information. I knew that he also stole recent documents. He was my friend. I had to 'play crazy' about this whole thing."

"Who is T.J.?"

"My ex-best friend now. Considering he's dead. He put me in a real bind."

"Can't you just go and say hey, T.J. did this, this and this? And they will let you go?"

"No it's not that easy."

"Why?"

"Because I hid money in my accounts for him. I just thought he was hiding it from the many women or more so people that he owed money to. Plus I was given a 'cut' a few times and if they really trace everything – they'll see that it was me. Now what I think is that someone knows this. They're pissed and they want revenge."

"So why not blame the next guy?"

"This happens to be me."

"Since he's dead..."

"Exactly. What I was hoping was that it would die with him."

"However, it's just the opposite."

"Yeah."

"I didn't know that."

"You wouldn't have."

"OK. I'm in."

"Good. You have two days to pack. We pushed up the date and were very fortunate. I'm so glad that you chose to."

"Somehow... So am I."

Adam is sitting at the table drinking a cup of coffee. His heart is heavy. The look on his face is unnerving. Cynthia walks in and notices the look. She stands over him and gives him a slight hug while kissing him on the forehead.

Mom's Loyalty

Adam is the first to speak. "Good morning baby."

"Good morning. I know that look. Which of the kids is it?"

"Look at this and you tell me."

He hands her the note in the evidence bag.

"Is that the note from the crime scene?"

"Yeah. What else?"

Cynthia reads the note out loud. "It sounds personal."

"Yep. What else?"

"I think that they are reaching out and no one is responding."

"OK and what else?"

"I don't know. I'm not the detective you are."

He hands her another evidence bag. "Now. What else?"

"That's... No it can't be. Is it?"

"So you tell me what to do."

"Honey you can't for so many reasons."

"It's my job."

"Job or not that's still your baby, your child."

"And what am I to do? I have to turn over evidence."

Cynthia is hysterical. "No you don't. I don't know. Something other than that?"

"You don't understand."

"NO! You don't understand. THAT IS MY BABY! How dare you?!"

"Don't do anything crazy. If you saw this then so did someone else. Which means that they know too. Hell. Two of my guys saw it when they handed it to me. It has to be done."

"Damn you Adam! Damn you and your job!"

Cynthia runs out of the room and up the stairs to make a call. She frantically sends out the text: LOOK. YOUR FATHER KNOWS! GET ON THE PLANE!!! As she presses send Adam walks in. She places her phone back in her purse. He looks at her in anger and disgust and storms out of the house. She breathes a sigh of relief.

Adam is in the car. For the first time ever he cries. He knows what he has to do and now he has to move fast because the window for everything is closing fast. He knows he should call for back up, but he can't stand the thought of the humiliation. Fortunately for him, the traffic is light and Derrick does not live too far away. He pulls up in the drive way. Derrick's car is there. He walks up to the door and notices that it is open. He draws his weapon and steps in.

The basement is dark and dank. There is only enough light to make out the figure in front of him. Adam is in and out of focus. At his moment of clarity he sees and recognizes the person in front of him. He can't move and his chest is tight.

"Well daddy, ain't this something for ya'? I guess you were too smart for your own good. You really should've let her handle her business and you wouldn't've been in this predicament." (He laughs.) "It wasn't meant for you to take over. She was supposed to get the glory. You stripped her of that. What kind of father are you? You have to always be in the spotlight. Well, (he moves the light closer in on Adam) I'm gonna give you the spotlight and let you think about what you have done here. Oh. And while you're thinking. As I know your one fear. (He drops a snake on his lap.) I hope he doesn't bite." (He Laughs.) "I wouldn't move if I were you. Before I go. How does it feel to lose? How does it feel to know that you are going to die? How does it feel to have your dignity stripped from you? Won't be yelling too much soon now wills ya? Only thing I regret – is not doing this sooner!"

Adam is muffled. "You son of a bitch! How could you. Who the hell do you think you are?"

"What. What was that?" (Leans in.)

"I'm the one that lives."

Once a Cop Always a Cop

Alana walks into the police station. Her old desk is just as she left it. Finley is standing over it looking over some papers. Everyone stops what they are doing when they see her walk in. Some walk up to greet her. There is general conversation between them. She continues to walk up to Finley.

"So. Guess who finally decides to come in?"

"Yeah well there were some things going on."

"Oh yeah?"

"Yep."

"So when are you going to explain that rock on your hand? While you are out there living a free life and playing girlfriend/boyfriend obviously – some of us have been working very hard. Especially with the new sheriff in town."

"My daddy?"

"As if you had to ask. Which, by the way, your mom called. She says that he went to see your brother and never returned?"

She shrugs her shoulders. "I don't know. Maybe he's having a moment."

"Yeah but she also said that it's unlike him not to check in."

"Not at all?"

"Nope."

"Anything else?"

"Oh and she said that he knows. Whatever that means."

"Oh my God."

There is a long pause.

"What? What?!"

"Look let's go. It's about to get deep."

"I'll drive."

"We have to get to Alex."

They leave the station in a hurry. Finley opens the door for Alana. They continue the conversation in the car while headed over to the M.E.

"You have to tell me everything you know. Maybe I can help."

"You are such a good friend. Here it is from the beginning. Early on, I suspected some activity and knew that everything wasn't right with my brother. I chalked it up to Terry's death and all. Then I saw some papers on his desk at home that looked very peculiar. I was impressed at first but then realized that this was stuff from work."

"OK it's not unusual to take stuff home especially for him."

"Yeah, but this time it's different."

"Different how?"

"I started putting two and two together. The first victim – Laura – she was an old girlfriend of his from high school before Lisa. Both of them broke his heart. First, Laura ditched him for T.J. and Lisa dumped him right before prom because she wanted kids right after graduating and he wanted to wait. So she got with this older dude and he took her through the ropes. She ended up waiting to have kids. And guess what? If she would have done it the way he wanted, that would have been his child."

"Oh crap."

"Yeah and it gets deeper. T.J. was having him hide money and even cut him in on some of the deals. At first it was nothing until things got real deep. So to try and cover it up – no more T.J."

"He really has patience."

"Oh I know."

"So explain the professor and the rich guy's wife."

"The professor failed him or at least attempted to because Derrick is so smart. I mean really smart. There's some stuff that I never told you that I think you should know too but I'll get to that in a minute. The rich guy, Mr. Lingerman, has a mistress. His wife knew but never said anything until recently and asked for a divorce taking a great deal with her. Well, he really wouldn't have the money to splurge on his mistress. And he's definitely not letting that kind of money go. So it's the easiest way to get rid of the wife. He is like a dad to Derrick. So Derrick would do whatever he asks because he really did treat him like his son. More than my own father. Don't get me wrong. My dad was there for us at all costs to him but he pushed us and pushed us to excellence."

"Is that such a bad thing?"

"No not really. But it was brutal growing up even though we were happy kids. We always had to look for his approval."

"Like that's changed."

"Right."

"OK what about the news caster and the homeless person."

"He has a degree in chemistry and psychology. It's all about the mind when it comes to him. I think they were just random. To throw things off."

"We're here."

They get out of the car and walk in. Alex tries to cut them off but he's too late. She sees her father lying on the table.

"Alana, no don't."

Alana, begins sobbing. She turns her head looking to Alex for comfort, "Alex"?

Alex walks up to her and wraps his arms around her in an intimate hug.

"Alana. Listen."

"To what?" (She covers her mouth to stifle her cry.) "Oh my God."

Finley steps around them to get a better view of the body. "Why weren't we contacted?"

Alex lets Alana go and they step closer to Adam's body.

"It wasn't your district where they found the body."

"Who?" Finley furrows his brow.

"West Sector."

"How?"

"Same old motive."

"What?" Alana sobs.

Finley turns his attention to Alana. "We need to talk more."

She sobers up just enough to have an audible conversation. "Well now that the gangs all here. I think it's my brother."

Alex's face turns up. "Oh God. No. Really?"

"Yes."

"That's what you meant earlier."

"Yeah."

"That's why you quit."

"Yeah. I knew a little more than I wanted to. We always talked about it and everything but I never knew the extent until now."

"So what are you going to do?"

"I don't know."

"They are on their way to tell your mom. You have to get there. You have to be there to be strong for her."

"Alex. This is going to kill her."

Finley walks up behind her and places his hand on her shoulder.

"You gotta come back. It will look bad if someone else arrests your brother. I suggest after the funeral. No one else knows but us."

"He's right Alana."

"Guys. I don't know. It's still going to be a scene. Have you thought about it? He kills my dad and I arrest him. Really?"

"What other options do you have?"

"Flight."

"Then you will be an accomplice."

"As a cop and your friend, I'm going to pretend that I didn't hear that."

"Didn't plan on coming back anyway."

"And what about your mom?"

"She can come with us. Everything is simple and easy. Just drop and go. Not even worrying about a funeral."

Finley pauses in bewilderment. "That's harsh even for you."

Alex already planning his life ahead with her and actually liking the idea of leaving. What comes out next is cryptic enough. "Alana. You know what you have to do."

"Easier said than done. (Walks over to her father. Whispers.) I'm so sorry."

"Again, as a cop my lips are sealed until after the funeral and then after that – if you can't I will. He still has to answer for what he has done."

"You're right."

"Good luck you two."

Alana and Finley leave. She glances back one more time. She wonders if he noticed the ring on her finger. Once in the car Finley turns on the sirens and high tails it. It is almost evening. Cynthia is pacing the floor. Something is bothering her really terribly. Alana and Finley walk through the door.

"We beat them. Good. Mom?"

"In here baby."

"Hey, what's going on?"

"It's your father."

"I know. There's something I need to tell you."

"Have you heard from your brother?"

"Not yet but mom."

"When do you plan on hearing from him?"

"Soon. Mom."

"Listen, your father knows it's him. Y'all have to leave and leave soon."

"I know. But Mom." She leaves the doorway. In her mind she's trying to find the words.

"Your father is going to be upset that I told you but I can't let anything happen to my babies."

"Told me what?"

"Your brother is a murderer."

"I already know mom. I figured that out a long time ago."

"And you didn't say anything?"

"He's my brother. What could I say?"

"Well your father is probably busy. I haven't heard from him and I haven't seen it on the news yet so it won't be long."

"You haven't watched the news at all?"

"No. I didn't turn on anything. I didn't want to hear it or see it."

Finley steps up closer. He's not quite in between but he's definitely within earshot. *"Tell her."*

"Tell me what?"

"I'm so sorry mom. Dad..." (She throws up. She grabs her stomach and falls on the couch.) "Oh my God."

"I'll get some towels."

"Are you okay?"

"I don't know where that came from."

"It's your nerves. You were like that as a kid too."

"Probably so."

"What were you saying?"

(Finley walks in with the towels and begins cleaning up the mess and hands a glass of water to Alana.)

"It's about dad." (The doorbell rings.)

"Hold on honey." She pats her hand and heads toward the door.

Cynthia opens the door. It is Chief Williams, Chief Walker and Detective Turner. Cynthia becomes ill and sick to her stomach. Alana is trying to get off the couch but she is dizzy.

Cynthia bellows out. "Oh God. No. No. No. No. No. No. Don't you dare! Don't you dare stand there and stare me in the face and tell me something is wrong with my husband. Don't you dare do it!"

"Mom!"

"Damn it. Alana. Why? Why he…"

"Mom!"

(Everyone looks around the room at each other wondering what is going on.)

Alana finally musters the energy to get up from the couch. "Look guys. I'll handle it."

Chief Williams is a little rough when he speaks. "But you're not on the force."

"I'm back. You just didn't know it yet. I am leading up the investigation and I have everything under control. I have a suspect. Either way, I will let you know." (She throws up again.)

Chief Walker from the West Side jumps back in time to keep from being vomited on. "Are you okay?"

"Yeah, I just need something salty like a pretzel or cracker." (She walks off to go get cleaned up.)

Chief Walker reaches his hand out to Cynthia. "I know this is a lot to deal with so we will leave you alone for now. Besides your daughter is here and I know you are in good hands. If you need anything of course you know how to reach me."

"Of course. Thanks." (She leads them out the door.)
"Alana?!"

"I'm in the bathroom."

"I'm coming in."

"It's not like you haven't seen me before."

Finley looks nervous as he knows what that means. "I'm just. I'm just going to stand by the door."

"Whatever."

Cynthia is ringing her hands together. There are light tears streaming down her face. "My Lord what am I going to do?"

"We have to play this cool. At least until after the funeral."

"I texted your brother a message. I don't think I should have done that."

Alana furrows her eyebrows. "When?"

"Yesterday."

"Not the best move but not too damaging either. Do you know if daddy talked to anyone?"

"No."

"No you don't or no he didn't."

"No he didn't."

"Good so far."

"Can you save your brother?"

"I'm going to try."

"Don't get yourself into trouble."

"I won't. I know what you shouldn't know."

"Thank you baby. Your father is gone."

"I know."

Finley walks up looking at his watch.

"I know that you guys are leaving and I'm down for keeping the family together but you don't have a lot of time."

"Right. You need to have the funeral like yesterday. Our plane leaves in 2 days."

"OK."

"Don't talk to the press or anyone else for that matter. How did dad find out?"

"Through the notes that he left. Right after you quit."

"Notes? What notes?"

"There were like 2 or 3 notes that he left. Handwriting matched to a "t"."

"Impossible."

"I'm ya momma. I know y'all more than anyone else."

"I didn't know."

Finley comes closer to the door. Alana is still getting cleaned up. He notices her figure. "That's why I asked you to meet me. There was a lot to discuss."

"I'm sorry. I just got tied up."

Cynthia does a double take forgetting that her husband is dead. She perks up as she sees the ring. "So what's with the ring?"

"I'm engaged to John. I'm trying to convince him to leave with me as Derrick is with Hannah."

"How did I miss all of this?"

"Things just kinda took off."

"So is there room for one more on that plane?"

"I was thinking the same thing, mom. I didn't want you to be alone. So Fins what else do you know?"

"Uh really nothing compared to what you just told me. You still have to explain the reporter."

"Again. I don't know that's so random." (She quietly thinks.) "Disrespect."

"What?"

"Yeah think about it. She talked about how the professor was a great man and all that. How he served on many boards and jury duty and stuff like that. She said that this was heinous and horrible blah, blah, blah. You know how reporters are."

"And the homeless person?"

"My brother? That's just random. Total test subjects to see how far he can go."

"Apparently too far."

Cynthia stands there. She is so confused and yet taking it all in.

"What else?"

Cynthia chuckles. Alana is so like her father.

"Besides the notes, that's really it. Your dad was starting to put some pieces together but that's all he knew."

Cynthia clears her throat. "He asked me about it yesterday and I about fell over."

"Man, why would Derrick do this?"

"There is no clear real motive other than what you said." Finley confirms her suspicions.

"I just can't believe my son! Why or what reason does your brother have for doing the things that he has done?"

Why do most people do anything?" Alana pulls out her shirt. "Mom you have to get over to Alex. Tell him to prep to send dad over to the funeral home. We have to move and quickly."

"I'll get right on it."

"Fins let's go we got other stuff to do."

"Right. (Hugs Cynthia.) Bye Momma Cynt."

"Bye honey. Be careful you two."

"Of course."

Alana grabs her coat and leaves.

Derrick and Hannah are at her place packing a few things. It was just as he imagined. It was small, cozy and quaint. Just enough for her. At the same time, she really didn't own much. So why was she so hesitant about leaving? He just turned on his cell phone. The messages are coming through. His phone beeps and vibrates with every message. He laughs. His phone never has had this much activity when it is on. But it's the last text message grabs him. Hannah looks up in time to see his face.

Love Birds

"What honey? What's wrong?"

"My father is looking for me."

"Why?"

"Lead Detective."

"So then we better move."

"Not yet. Something's wrong."

"Why?"

"He's not here."

"OK Well maybe he's waiting for a warrant or something."

"You don't know my father."

"Well from what you told me... Besides he doesn't know about me."

"It's deeper than that. He's like super cop or something. The man can smell fear like a lion or something. He should have been here by now. We can't hide from him. There are eyes and ears everywhere."

"Well, this is your chance."

"I gotta call Alana. (He dials her number. At the same time she knocks on the door.)

"Open the door."

(Derrick jumps up and opens the door.)

"Hey Finley. Where's John?"

"He's home."

"What's the deal?"

"Dad is... (Takes a deep breath.) Dad's dead."

"Oh."

"I saw his body Derrick. We need to talk."

"About what? We have other things to be concerned with."

"I know."

(Hannah looks at Derrick as to why he is not so concerned.)

"Oh my God. Are you guys okay?" Her concern is still overlooked.

"No, everything is not ok." Alana speaks with great irritation. Although she has Alex and John; she can't help but be jealous of Derrick's intimacy with her.

"Anything I can do to help?"

"Yeah. Stay out of the way for now. Derrick get dressed now. We're leaving."

"Where are we going?"

Hannah steps up, "What about me?"

Alana is irritated and looks her up and down. "What about you? Right now my only concern is my brother."

(Hannah scoffs.)

Finley tries to diffuse the situation and reassure Hannah. "Look, it is deep. Real deep! Right now you have to really trust your sister."

Alana turns her back to walk out the door. "Hurry up. We're going to the morgue."

"Alright."

(Hannah sits on the couch and waits for their return. Meanwhile they all pile in the car to meet Cynthia.)

"Detective, what's the game plan?" Finley breaks the silence.

"Get dad buried as soon as possible. Derrick. Imma need just a little bit more emotion from you."

"What do you mean?"

"Just a little more sadness than just 'okay'. I know he wasn't your favorite person, but he's still your father."

"Considering all that's going on, what do you expect? You act as if I wanted him dead. (She shoots him a glance.) Baby, I love you and the family. But the truth is – it is part of the job. I expect the same from you too."

(This time Finley shoots him a glance.)

"Wow. Is there something I'm missing?"

Alana totally ignores Finley. "I know but hopefully it won't go that far."

Finley – feeling the need to say something, "Yeah hopefully."

Alana turns to completely face Derrick. "We need to move on this and be on our toes."

"So what?"

"At the funeral you shed a tear or two. Make sure you stand by mom and hold her hand."

"I know what to do."

"Yeah but at the same time."

"Hold on. Wait a minute. Do you really believe it was me?"

"Derrick. I believe you are involved somehow. And guess what? So will a whole bunch of other people. We don't know if dad talked to anybody or not and there's a lot of chances and things that we just can't afford to take."

"I'm sorry. I messed up."

"I know. But I'm gonna clean it up for you."

(They simultaneously meet up with their mom and enter the morgue.)

Derrick is happy to see Cynthia. "Mom." He hugs her tightly.

"Boy where have you been?! I've been worried sick about you."

"I was with Hannah and we were spending quality time together."

"Things have really taken off with you and Alana. Unbelievable. Well, I guess I can be happy that you all are in happy, healthy relationships."

Alana scoffs. "If that's what you wanna call it."

"I'm sorry about dad."

"I know. Look right now what we need to do is think about saving our family."

(They walk in together.)

Alex looks up from Adams body placing the last stitch. "Well, hello. I'm sorry to be meeting on such bad terms."

Alana speaks sarcastically. "When have they ever been good?"

Alex returns with a sarcastic, seductive reply. "If you would stick around then you would know."

"Mmmm. I just might. (Derrick shoots her a killer glance of jealously. Finley and Cynthia are thoroughly confused.) Look. I need your help. How quickly can you process my dad and get him to the funeral parlor."

"For you? It's done."

"Thanks."

Derrick visibly disturbed by their banter. "Yeah thanks."

(Alex walks over and hugs Cynthia as she sobs uncontrollably.)

"The good news of it all is he didn't suffer. That much I do know."

"That's comforting to know."

Alana begins to cry. "Daddy." (Before anyone can reach her, Derrick pulls her in his arms and rubs her back.)

Finley speaks quietly. "Interesting."

(Alex looks on in confusion.)

Finley drops everyone back off at Cynthia's place. He goes back to the station and sits at his desk. He is looking very perplexed when Chief Williams walks up to him.

"Finley. Finley."

He snaps out of his thought. "Yeah Chief? What's up?"

"Why do you look like your brain is about to melt down?"

"Huh? Oh. Nothing."

"There's something."

"I've just been thinking."

"About what?" (Another officer joins the conversation.)

"Moral and ethical dilemmas."

The Officer speaks solemnly. "Those can be the toughest decisions."

"Tell me about it."

Chief Williams moves on, not seeming too concerned. "What do you know?"

Officer Hoffman is a portly fellow and has been around for a very long time. Finley often looks to him for advice. Before Finley answers the Chief, Hoffman throws up a chubby hand.

"Before you answer that. Where do your loyalties lie?"

"Who said it had to do with the job?"

"You just did."

(Chief Williams gives them a stern look.)

Finley proceeds with caution. "Look Chief. I need to talk to you...   Alone."

(They walk into the Chief's office. There are papers everywhere. The Chief shuts the door.)

"Level with me."

"First is Wells really back?"

"Between me and you. I never let her go. I knew she would be back. She just needed some time off."

"I had a feeling that was the case."

"So what has you so perplexed?"

"Chief I have to tell you this in confidence."

"What does this have to deal with?"

"You already know."

"Then what am I missing?"

"It's her brother. There are some crazy weird connections to everyone except the homeless person. That was just random."

"And what does she say?"

"Truthfully, she's torn."

"As I would imagine."

"Really? Can you imagine arresting your own brother?"

"If he had broken the law? Yes."

"I tell you what. You need to talk to her before tomorrow."

"Why?"

Finley walks out the door. "Airplanes."

"Shit."

(He picks up the phone and calls Wells. She answers on the first ring.)

"Hello?"

"Hey look. I need you to come in so that we can talk. When can you get here?"

She walks through the door of his office. "Now."

"Wow. Some time off changes a person."

"I know. It hasn't been that long."

"Long enough. So how are you holding up?"

"As good as to be expected."

"Good to see you back."

"Can't say it's good to be back."

"Under the circumstances, I do understand. We have a lot to cover."

"Where to start?"

"First I never took you off payroll. I just put you on stress leave. No one knows it but me. So don't go telling anybody. Second, I understand that you are leaving after your father's funeral. Is this so?"

"Yes."

"How is that possible?"

"I only came back because of my father and to help Finley. My original plan to leave remains the same."

"I can use all the help I can get and I know now that this is personal for you.

"Yeah it is. More than you know."

"Anything I can do to be of assistance?"

"Not really. There are some things that I have to iron out."

"Just remember that your job is your job and your ethics are your ethics. I have faith that you will do the right thing."

"Don't I always?"

"Well, I will let you get to work and let me know what you come up with."

"Will do."

(She leaves his office and goes over to her desk.)

Finley is anxious and nervous not knowing what was said. "Well, what's the deal?"

"I don't know. I haven't put everything together yet. What are you going to do?"

"I got your back no matter which way you go."

"You have always been such a good friend and partner to me."

"Don't say that too loud because then everybody would expect equal treatment."

Alana laughs. "You are too much."

"Anyway, let's do some police work and get the hell out of here."

He leads her towards the door.

Alana stretches. "Like there's any work to be done."

"I know. I just wanted to get out so that we could talk."

"Dang. I didn't catch that one."

They go for a long walk to get out of earshot of anyone who could be listening.

"So your mom is coming with you guys?"

"Yeah."

"What about all your stuff?"

"I have someone taking care of all that."

"You know you should do the right thing. "

"I know but the right thing this time is so hard."

"You have to trust yourself."

"How?"

"I don't know. That one you have to figure out yourself."

"Why this? Why now?"

"To test you."

"By whom?"

"The powers that be, maybe? Whatever deity that you pray to?"

"Yeah but I lived a good life so I don't know what I did to warrant this."

"Sometimes it's just to test your strength and faith."

"Yeah."

"So the funeral is tomorrow. You guys really move quick."

"You already know what's on the line."

"Yeah. I just realized the position you put me in."

"Huh?"

"Nothing. Look I got some thinking to do. I'll see you at the funeral."

"OK."

Alana makes it back to her apartment. John is there with her. She's lying on the couch and wondering. John walks out of the bathroom. He leans over and begins kissing her lightly all over.

Oops

"Penny for your thoughts?"

"How many do you have?"

"Whatever you need."

"I just have some real deep stuff that's going on and I'm not so sure honestly how to handle it."

"Well for now. Let's NOT think about it. Tomorrow is the funeral and then we leave so no worries real soon."

"If only it were that simple."

"It can be if you just let it. Look let's go to bed. You need to get your rest. There's a long day ahead for all of us."

"OK. On one condition."

"What's that?"

"You hold me all night and tell me how much you love to be with me."

"My pleasure."

They enter the bedroom to sleep. Time passes and he begins to rub her legs and arms.

Alana in a deep sleep state. "Oh Derrick."

"What?" John sits up then lays back down.

Time to Grieve

It is the day of the funeral. The morning is very gloomy. The sun is barely shining. Alana's phone rings. It's Finley.

"Hey."

"I have some bad news and I need you at the morgue."

"For what? You do know my father's funeral is today?"

"For what? Like always – it's about work."

"Again. You do realize what today is?"

"Yes and if you hurry we can still make it."

"I'm on my way."

John stands in front of her with his hands on his hips.

"Really you're going to work today?"

"It is my job."

"That you are quitting in less than 8 hours."

"Well until then I still have to do my part. You can come if you wish."

"Do I have a choice?"

She smiles sweetly and intently at him. "No."

(They leave and head to the morgue. They pull up to the morgue and see officers all around. Finley walks up to her.)

Finley catches up to her first. "I want to tell you something."

Alana feels panicked. Her chest tightens. She knows something is wrong. "What? What? Where's Alex?"

"Wells. Alex's... Uh... Well."

Alana breaks. "Finley. Don't."

"I'm so sorry."

Alana falls to her knees. "God! Why?!"

Her screaming startles John. He doesn't know whether or not to get out of the car. He decides to stay.

Finley picks her up. "Look. I need you to head this up for me and I'll do the other stuff and meet you at the funeral in a bit. Um, one thing. (Whispers.) Where's Derrick? Where has he been in the last few hours?"

"I, I don't know."

"Wells. Alex? Why?"

"It wasn't him. It can't be."

"It was easy to cover when it was your dad, but he's really put himself out there now."

"What am I gonna do?"

"What you're supposed to."

"But it's my brother for Christ sakes."

"Brother or not – he's broken the law."

"Oh God. Why me?"

"Why not you? Pull yourself together. We have a crime scene to process."

She collects herself. She takes a deep breath and walks in to see Alex's body on the table with a note next to it. She grabs a pair of gloves to pick up the note.

She reads the note:

*"Glad to see that you are back. I need a
challenge in my life. Sorry about 'that man'
and your friend. Ok. Well not about 'that
man' but I just get a little jealous sometimes.
Love Bug"*

Finley feeling defeated. "So that's it."

"I guess so."

"Mental note it and I'll see you later."

"Done."

(She walks back to the car. She is crying heavily as she gets into the car.)

"Honey, what's wrong? What is it?"

"It's Alex. He's dead. He's been a longtime friend for ages. He's dead. On the day they bury my father. All I need to lose is my brother too."

"Don't say that. In a few hours this will be a distant memory. So much so – you won't remember that it even happened."

(She throws up.)

"Oh my God."

"It's your nerves. You'll be okay."

"That is so gross."

"Aw it's nothing. Let's swing by, get you cleaned up and end this nightmare."

"It's just beginning."

(Wells starts the car and pulls off.)

Meanwhile at the funeral parlor. It is filled with many officers. Each officer and family member are making their way around greeting and consoling each other.

Chief Williams is in full uniform. "Cynt – I'm so sorry."

"That's ok. Thank you so much for being here."

"As if I would be anywhere else."

"You don't think we're in any danger."

Chief Williams looks around and smirks. "In this place – at this time? Nah. Where is Derrick?"

He asked a little too eagerly for her liking.

"He's taking it a bit hard but I think he will be here."

"There are some things that I have to ask you once this is over."

"No. Ask me now."

"I don't think this is the appropriate time."

"When it comes to me and my family, I don't care what time it is."

"Well Cynt – to be honest some things have been brought to my attention and I have to address them."

Cynthia raises her eyebrow. "Like what?"

"They say it's Derrick and it only makes sense when you put it all together."

"And where did you get your information from?"

"Does it matter?"

"Hell yeah it matters. This is my baby and family that's being destroyed here."

"Cynt calm down. Let's not make a scene."

"Let's not make a scene? You took it there. How do you think I'm supposed to react when you come to me with this craziness on the day I bury my husband who lost his life because of you?"

"My source is reliable."

"You need to pin this on someone and my son is the logical choice? Is that all you got? What evidence do you have?"

"Let's not go there. I've gotten convictions on less than that."

Cynthia sneers and moves in close to him about to go off. "Let me tell you something." (Interrupted. She sees Derrick walk up.)

"Mom."

"Hey baby. How are you?"

"Considering."

"I know baby. (She hugs him tight.) Where's your sister?"

"She threw up again, but she's on her way."

"And Hannah?"

"Here." He points to Hannah as she walks up.

She immediately hugs Cynthia. "Mother Wells."

"Baby, just call me mom."

"Yes Ma'am."

Chief Williams is a little embarrassed. "Cynthia I will talk to you later."

"No. You won't."

Chief Williams walks away. She shoots him a very nasty glance.

Hannah waits until the Chief leaves and then whispers, "He knows?"

"Yeah but don't worry."

Alana and John are heading back to the funeral. They are talking in the car.

"You know what you have to do?"

"I know! Why does everyone keep *saying* that!! I'm just so angry."

"You really can't be mad at him."

"The hell I can't. He took our father. We probably could have worked out something."

"Is it you are just angry over your father?"

"What is that supposed to mean?"

"Nothing. So what are you going to do? You really have to consider doing the right thing."

"I don't know. That's the only thing I really know I guess. (Just then she gets a text. She reads it.) Shit!"

"What?"

"The press was just alerted."

"Who would snitch?"

"I don't know but I have to let them know and move quickly."

"This is getting real ugly real fast."

"You're telling me?"

Wells flips on her lights and sirens. She blows through lights and signs to make it just in time to see the press are also pulling up. They all scramble with questions.

"They don't waste time do they?"

"No. No they don't."

Reporter #1: "Wells can we get a statement?"

Alana is irritated. "Yeah! How about – no comment."

Reporter #2: "Is it true you are close to the killer?"

"Whatever. Anyway, ladies and gentlemen, this is a private affair. I know how you love to cover stuff like this, (John wraps his arms around her.) but my family is grieving and some privacy would be nice. Besides, you are giving that S.O.B. more credit than he deserves."

She and John walk in and the officer on duty closes the door behind them and begins to waive everyone away.

Derrick sees her. He quickly walks up to her.

"Hey baby."

His arms wrapped around her waist.

"Hey. You good?"

"Yeah."

"It's thick out there."

"I saw. So how are we going to do this?"

"We gotta talk."

"Now?"

Alana shoots him a glance and they walk out of the service into the hallway. They leave Hannah and John standing there looking at each other as if to question their relationships to each other.

"Look, I have to do something I don't want to."

"What?"

"Something that my mind tells me to but my heart won't let me."

Derrick looks deep into her eyes and grabs her hand. "I understand."

"I understand what's going on but it has to be done. And if you let me do my job – it will be easy."

"Alana. I trust you."

"Before the repast, I must take you into custody."

"Poor little sis you just can't let it go can you?"

"It's my job and my duty to dad."

"He's dead now. Does it really matter?"

"Yeah. It does."

"Fine. But how are you going to explain this to everyone? What about Cape Verde?"

"I'll worry about that. You just need to cooperate. Better you are picked up by me than anyone else including Fins."

"Who tipped off the press?"

"I don't know but I damn sure aim to find out."

"Let's go back in before they get even more suspicious."

"By the way, why Alex?"

Just then Cynthia, John and Hannah come out of the door.

Cynthia gives them a stern, motherly look. "The funeral is about to start. Let's go."

They speak simultaneously. "Yes Ma'am."

The funeral procession goes on. Alana breaks down several times. It was an amazing sight to see. Derrick and John fighting over her. Cynthia and Finley look on in confusion. Chief Wells also got a few glimpses of the entire thing. It finally hit Derrick as they made the final round to say good bye and he bursts into tears. Hannah quickly and swiftly comes to his side. Alana was wrapped into John's arms and she said nothing.

The funeral procession finally made it to the grave site. Derrick is standing in between Alana and Cynthia. He has his arm around Alana's waist rubbing it and holding his mother's hand. The tears are flowing from all of their faces. While The Three Volley Salute is completed Finley walks off to get the car and the flag is passed to Cynthia. She presses it up against her chest. As everyone is walking away, Finley pulls up in an unmarked car followed by two patrolmen to arrest Derrick. Alana waives him off as to say that she is handling it and he stands back. Derrick is in front of her and he just bows his head in shame.

Once everyone leaves, Alana begins giving Derrick his Miranda Rights. Chief Williams stands in the background astonished and proud that she chose her job over her brother. **They** *are watching.*

Alana pulls out her cuffs. Derrick turns around without a fight. "Derrick Allen Wells, you have the right to remain silent. Anything you say can and will be used against you in the court of law. You have the right to an attorney. If you cannot afford one – one will be appointed to you. Do you understand the rights that have been presented to you?"

Derrick chuckles. "Yeah I do."

Alana places him in the squad car. The press is constantly snapping shots and reporting back to their respective stations. Alana throws up again.

"What's wrong with her?" Finley asks inquisitively.

"It's obvious. She's pregnant." Cynthia smirks.

"Oh my God."

"I know. My God too."

First Prison Visitor

As if things could not be any gloomier. The next few weeks doesn't get any better. Alana visits her brother at the Prisoner Holding Center. She checks in and leaves her weapon. He is sitting at a small table in the corner. Alana acknowledges the other officers in the room by giving each one a head nod. She sits down at the table.

"Hey you."

"Hey."

"How you holding up?"

He gestures around the room. "Considering."

"I know. Just give me more time. I *will* have you out in no time."

"That's what you said two weeks ago."

"There are still parts of the puzzle that I have to put together for them so that it fits just right."

"And then what?"

"You may have to do a year or two plus psych evaluations and then they will let you go."

"But I didn't do anything!"

"The evidence says you did."

"Basically, I have to play crazy to get out of this?"

"Basically."

"What was wrong with the original plan?"

"It would have been fine except for the information that was leaked and they would have been waiting. That's the first place they'd go."

"True. Just hurry up and do what you can."

"You know I will."

They hug and Alana leaves. He watches her and admires her from a far. There is a news cast on the radio. Female person is giving the update.

Prisoner: "Hey man, they talkin' 'bout you."

"Turn it up." He walks over to get a better listen.

The prisoner does as requested.

Radio: In lighter news since the arrest of suspect Derrick Wells, there has not been one murder and the city can sleep easy tonight. He's facing anywhere from a light sentence of 2-5 with probation to the death penalty. Although I can guess what most are hoping for. The horrific nature of the crime alone shocks the nation. It also brought to light that there are some unorthodox ways in the military and technology which is also now being investigated.

An officer walks in and turns off the radio.

Officer: "Lights out."

John's Little Secret

Alana makes it home. John has dinner cooking and the aroma is delightful. Her apartment is back to the lived in status. Everything is unpacked. John is sitting on the couch. As Alana is trapped in her thoughts – John startles her by sitting on the couch next to her.

"About time you got home."

"I had some things to do."

"Like go visit your brother?"

"Yeah. How did you know?

"Lucky guess. How you feeling?"

"Better today than yesterday."

"Well good. Here's a glass of wine baby. (Handing her the glass.) Come take a load off. (He pats the spot next to him.) Let your husband take care of you."

"Mmmmm. That would be nice. You are really loving that idea huh? Soon baby soon. And honestly I can't wait for the day."

John begins rubbing her shoulders as she takes a few sips of the wine. He begins whispering in her ear.

"You know. I love you but you would never be fully mine. And if I can't have you..."

"Baby, you know I am here for you but I have to be there for my family too."

"Hmph. I know. But ever since that night, I have been so angry at you."

"What are you talking about?"

"Some time ago you called Derrick's name instead of mine when I rubbed you while you were sleeping."

"Honest mistake I guess. I have had a lot on my mind."

"Really? I'm going to ask you one last time. What is the deal between you and your brother?"

"Ugh!" She grabs her head.

"What's the matter? Feeling a little woozy? Yep. That's how it starts."

She is growing dizzier. She is trying to form her words. "What? What are you talking about?"

"I have a little secret for you."

She retches. "What"

He whispers. "It wasn't your brother."

(She passes out)

Alana is tied to the chair. She is bound and gagged. She is still feeling out of it. She is unable to control her senses. Her sight is coming into focus. She sees John.

Alana's Fate is Sealed

"Hey Babe. Confused? I'll give you the low down. This is how Darmstadtium works. It's odorless and colorless. It's borderline between a metal and a gas. Just as soon as you see it – it's gone. But you already knew that."

Through her muffle, "Yooouuuuu!!"

"Yeah. Me. Now. Couple that with a few other chemicals and boom! You can use it as a truth serum or a torture device. Or in your case both. (He lights up a cigarette.) You smell that? It's gas. You tell me the truth and I let you live – lie and you die. (She looks at the machines beeping.) That? Oh that's my own little version of a polygraph so try to lie if you want to. It detects everything. First question, (pulling off the gag) How close are you and your brother?"

"Close."

"Intimate close?"

"No." The machine beeps.

"Liar!" He slaps her so hard, the sound echoes off the walls.

He then burns her with the cigarette.

Alana screams in pain. "I swear."

"The machine says different."

"I need. I need to tell you something."

"The only thing you need to tell me is what I want to know."

"NO. You need to listen!"

"NO. YOU LISTEN! I love you. I have always loved you since high school. You know it should have been me and you. Why do you think I did all this? It wasn't your brother – it was me because he had everything else and still he took you away from me! I can't get over you Alana! Why can't you see that? Why can't you understand that?"

"Look, whatever you've done - undo. I'M PREGNANT!"

"What?! Why didn't you say something?"

"I JUST DID! Please stop this. I just found out. Besides I didn't think my future husband would try and kill me."

John sneers. "I didn't think my *future wife* would still have such an intimate relationship with her brother."

"He's NOT my brother! Biologically anyway. And I keep telling you – it's not like that."

"Liar!"

"It's true! It's true! God! I'm telling you the truth."

John screams out in anger.

Alana cries. "Please don't kill our baby."

"Shut up! It's too late. It has to be done."

"What?! Please!"

Finley steps into view. He stares at her menacingly. His eyes are dark and cold.

"Yeah Wells. It has to be done."

"Fins. What is this? What is going on?"

Finley grabs her hair and pulls her head back. "You really don't think I played second chair to you for no reason?"

Alana is falling in and out as the serum takes effect. "Fins how could you?"

"Simple. You of all people should know how these things go. Pick your poison. Oh let's say money, revenge – things of that nature. Untie her. Let her go out with a little honor."

John does as he is told and unties her.

"Finley. I'm pregnant."

"What does that mean to me? Hmmmm. Let's see. Oh. I got. That's right. Nothing. It's not my baby. I never fucked you although, you do like to get around. John here. Alex. Derrick."

John turns around in anger. "What?!" He runs up to her and punches her in the jaw. She falls to the floor.

"Easy tiger. We can't be leaving lots of marks. It's called evidence. Go outside and cool off."

"Money maybe. But revenge? What did I do to you?" She holds her stomach.

"You were married once right? Guy named Treston? Ring a bell?"

"He was abusive and he tried to kill me."

"But you got the better hand huh? You screwed him up so bad that he killed himself. And no matter what – he's still my brother and you took him from me. So that's kinda the revenge part plus you took my position. You and *dad* thought you were hot shit. And guess what. YOU GOT PLAYED! (Laughs heartily.) You think this was all coincidence? I knew a long time ago what your brother and T.J. were up to from every move they have ever made. The both of you were so calculated. All roads lead to your brother because *I* made it that way."

Alana spits out blood. "Are you serious?"

"Well thanks to John. He helped to set it up nicely."

"No problem." John begins setting up a fire.

"You see that? Soon the effects will begin to burn off and you will feel this literally. That's the pain I felt when you left me on this earth alone."

"It was okay for him to do those things to me?"

"You could have just left."

"I tried and TWICE and he tried to kill me. TWICE!"

"You could have made it if you wanted to."

"Why set up my brother?"

"Everyone has to hurt. Besides I never liked him in school anyway."

"Huh?"

"Oh come now. Me, John and your brother all went to school together. You don't remember? Hence John liked you – more like obsessed with you and your brother just wouldn't let him get next to you until now which was perfect."

"Yeah. Just perfect." John chuckles menacingly.

"Looks like you have just bad luck or bad taste in men."

"You're crazy."

"Yes and I love all my crazy. And the money? I was already investigating T.J. and your brother's name came up and that's when I knew he had a lil sumtin' sumtin' to do with it. Y'know wut I mean? (Chuckles.) So I sent a message to your brother to which he basically ignored and so me being the "G" that I am – I decided to go with the original plan. And boy is it sweet! You and your Poppa never saw it coming. I beat the great Wells family at their own game. Ha! Imagine that!"

"You took my father away from me over some BS?"

"Oh I didn't do that one. Johnny boy did that. For you. (Laughs.) I'm telling you he would do anything for you."

John scoffs. "Not anymore. I stand to get a big inheritance. Didn't really want no kids anyway."

(He begins to tie her back and move her towards the fire.)

Alana too weak tries to jerk free. "You son of b..."

He slaps her again. "Ot, ot, ah. That is not the language of a lady. You don't speak badly of my mother. The wonderful woman she is."

John and Alana begin to tussle and struggle. Finley steps in and that's when Derrick walks through the door armed. He shoots several bullets towards Finley.

"Wow. And here I thought you had our backs."

Finley pulls his own gun. "Yeah, far back. Not one step closer or I'll put a bullet in this bitch's head."

John is high on his supply. "What a situation!"

"Derrick. They put the serum in me." Alana is close to passing out.

"Don't worry."

"Don't worry?! I'm pregnant! (She drops to the floor.) I don't feel so good. What took you so long?"

"A.J. (their brother, his identical twin) - hold on."

Alana screams in pain. "Why does it hurt?"

"It shouldn't. I think you are miscarrying."

John looks over at Alana and back to Derrick. "You're not the only smart one. I changed it. Made it better. Mr. Lingerman depends on me now. Besides, you're supposed to be in jail."

"You should have listened to her. She told you the truth."

Derrick sends two bullets into John. He drops to the floor. He takes one final look at Alana.

"Didn't know that Derrick was a twin huh? Die bitch!" She spits a large amount of blood into his face.

John takes one final breath not before Alana flips him the bird.

Finley steps off to the side and speaks back to Derrick.

"Yo! Thanks for doing my dirty work. John was a loose cannon getting high off his own supply."

"Now, before I kill you. Any last words?"

"First of all did you forget about who I am?"

"Nope – but I bet you forgot that I was a sharp shooter. You may be able to hit me, but I will definitely kill you.

"Oh I highly doubt that."

"Bug! How did you find me?"

"I kept calling your phone and you didn't answer – so I looked you up on GPS. I just had this feeling."

"Touching family moment, but I have to say it doesn't move me."

He moves in to shoot Alana when she stands up and pulls her gun. Finley sends off 3 simultaneous shots. One hits Derrick in the arm. Wells fires at Finley and hits him in the stomach, but not before Finley turns his attention on her and shoots her twice - once in the chest and the other in the stomach. Derrick drops to the floor. Finley mistakes this as Derrick being defeated. When he lowers his weapon, Derrick sends one bullet to his head. The same manner in which he was going to kill Alana.

The fire grows larger. Derrick musters up the energy to pick up Alana and carry her out of the building. She is bleeding profusely. He throws her in the car and speeds down the highway to the local hospital. He estimated that the blaze should be erasing all the evidence by now. He picks up his cell phone to call 911.

They finally make it to the hospital. Derrick screams for help. Nurses and orderlies rush to take Alana out of his arms and tend to him as well. Some time passes and Derrick calls Cynthia to let her know the news. Thirty minutes pass and Cynthia arrives with Hannah.

Derrick looks up from his bed. The first person he lays eyes on is – Hannah.

Cynthia speaks first, "Where is she?"

"She's in the operating room. I told them everything that they should know."

"The baby?"

Derrick shakes his head no and has a sad look on his face. She grabs her heart.

"Oh God."

"They say she should make it."

"Does she know?"

"I don't know what she knows right now."

A nurse walks in to take Derrick's vitals.

Cynthia turns to the nurse. "Do you know about my daughter? His sister that he came in with?

"Yes Ma'am"

"Will I be able to see her soon?"

The nurse puts on her best smile. "I believe once she is in the recovery room you will be able to."

"Good."

"Let me get his vitals and I will see what I can find out for you."

"Thank you."

Everyone settles in Derrick's room. Hannah is busy looking at her phone. Derrick is sleep. Cynthia is looking out the window and praying. Finally, the nurse comes in and announces that Alana is in the recovery room, but only one person is allowed to see her at a time. Cynthia leaves to see Alana. Alana is lying in bed. She has come to. She is flushed. The only thing Cynthia does is sit next to her, smiles and holds her hand.

The Truth Comes Out

Today the sun is shining and everyone has a smile on their face. They all meet up at the courthouse. Alana and Derrick are testifying against everything and everyone, but to also free their brother Adam Jr.

The D.A. Jocelyn Johnson is questioning Derrick. She is wearing a sharp Armoni suit. Her hair is pulled up in a bun and her skin is fair. Derrick is made to testify first.

"So according to the tape. This John West is responsible for all of the murders along with Detective Jason Finley?"

"Yes. There was this formula. It was mixed with Darmstadtium. It was ideal for warfare to obtain information from the subject in custody by ways of a truth serum. Its chemical base also affects the brain in which the intended victim thinks that they are dying given enough dosage. As they think they are dying, their body transitions to that particular kind of death."

"Remarkable. Did Mr. Lingerman put them up to it?"

"I honestly don't know. He's not that type of man. He was a father to me."

"What was your involvement?"

"I had no idea what was going on. I was just the Team Leader."

"So you have no idea of the depth of Mr. Lingerman's involvement?"

"No. All I know is that we were experimenting for the D.O.D. We had several contracts."

"What do you think happened?"

"Basically. It's chemical warfare. It works because whatever you imagine you can actually do it. For instance. Say that your subject or victim was injected. You can then in a hypnosis kind of way influence their mind to believe that they are dying. Once injected, you can put a gun to someone's head and pull the trigger. The eyes see the trigger being pulled and the brain knows that when a gun trigger is pulled and there is a bang a bullet must follow. The neurons in the brain tell you that you've just been shot in the head and therefore your body will react in the same manner. Thus _death by imagination_."

"What is your sister's involvement?"

"Detective Wells did not know anything about what was going on. In her eyes she thought I may have been guilty. In order to pull out the truth, we called in Adam Jr., my twin to arrest so that we could get to the truth. We all are really close. No one knew of Adam because he lived with my birth mother. That was the agreement between my mother and father. I am adopted. But we are still family. When Adam Jr. heard the news he called to see how he could help. That's when he flew into town to help; keeping a low profile."

"So how did you find your sister?"

"I found her through GPS. I had this feeling something wasn't right. I kept calling her. She wouldn't answer her phone. I knew then that I had to locate her. The last time that she didn't answer, her former husband had tried killing her also. I guess she just doesn't have good luck with men."

"Then what happened?"

"I made it shortly after they began torturing her. Words were exchanged and then gunfire. We made it to the hospital. She lost her baby and for a while she would not speak. I believe she has suffered psychologically a great deal. She honestly never knew a normal life. None of us have."

"Thank you. No further questions Your Honor."

There is a brief break before Alana is made to testify. They are kept separated as to not corroborate their stories.

"So it is in your professional opinion that Detective Finley and John West plotted this entire thing?"

Alana clears her throat. "Yes. Jason Finley and John West plotted to set up my brother Derrick Wells from long ago. The link between Derrick and the victims are true. Detective Finley used this to his advantage to murder the victims with the assistance of John West."

"So besides working together. How are you and Detective Finley connected?"

"I was married to Finley's brother in which I did not know at the time. His brother and I were having marital issues and when we divorced – he eventually killed himself. He thought my brother and I were the reason for his suicide. Finley also believed that for some odd reason, my brother was in with T.J. another worker for Lingerman Tech was making money from unscrupulous deals. To which this has never been proven."

"Why would a homicide detective investigate corporate fraud?"

Alana clears her throat, "He was very smart and good at following trails and putting pieces together."

"Finley wanted in on it as he was the lead investigator on the case. When Derrick did not give in because he was innocent, that's when he began plotting the murders with John. John was my recent fiancé."

The DA continues to question Alana's credibility. There is some doubt in her next question. "So how were you able to come up with the leads that you had?" She continues, "I analyzed all the information that my father and I gathered through the investigation and took a closer look at the notes and the motive. It seemed odd to me that suddenly the murderer would leave notes. My brother, even if he was capable of murder, knows better than to even leave a single trace of anything. I never really knew that John was in on it until the end when he tried to kill me."

"Who fired the first shot?"

"The very first shot came from Detective Finley and from there, shots were fired from everywhere."

"What are your professional findings?"

"It is my findings that Derrick Wells had nothing to do with T.J. White or Detective Finley although they knew each other outside of this. He was a pawn in a game of cat and mouse and I'm grateful that I was able to find the truth."

"How has this entire situation affected you psychologically?"

"I am coping. But it has not prevented me from doing my job or clouding my judgment."

"You arrested the wrong brother. Many people could see that as abuse of power or misjudgment."

"I had no intentions of causing harm. Adam Jr. knew he would not fare well in any altercation. I knew that I could trust Derrick, not only to protect me, but if push came to shove, he would serve his time. If it had not been done this way. I would be dead now."

"Yes. Indeed. It worked in you all's favor. Thank you. No further questions Your Honor."

The hours pass. It feels like eternity. The fate of the three siblings is now in the hands of the jury. It is late in the afternoon. Now that they have testified Cynthia is able to sit with Alana. They sit in silence, holding their breath. Cynthia continuously rubs Alana's hand. Alana wants to tell her that she's going to rub her skin off, but given the circumstances, she lets it slide. Hannah sits quietly staring at an odd spot on the wall. Derrick is sitting in a guarded holding room. Adam is sitting in a separate holding room.

A verdict has been reached. Everyone is sitting together. The two brothers are sitting side by side and the women are behind them. The jury files in and time seems to have stood still. Once they all are seated. The judge speaks.

The Verdict

"Ladies and gentleman of the jury. I would like to thank you for your time and assistance in this trial. Has the jury reached a unanimous decision without threat and being under duress?"

The Foreman stands.

"Yes your Honor."

"In the case of the People vs Adam Wells Jr. for Fraudulent Arrest. How do you find the defendant?"

"Not guilty."

"In the case of the People vs Derrick Wells for Murder in the First Degree. How do you find the defendant?"

"Not guilty."

"In the case of the People vs Derrick Wells for Money Laundering. How do you find the defendant?"

"Not guilty"

The entire time the room is silent. Not a sound could be heard.

"Detective Wells, Mr. Adam Wells and Mr. Derrick Wells. You all played a very dangerous game. There are rules for a reason. I hope you have learned to choose your associates wisely. You are free to go."

The moment the judge bangs his gavel, everyone lets out a sigh of relief. The guys turn to thank the lawyers for their hard work and then hug their family. Cynthia, Derrick, Adam and Alana are leaving the courthouse holding hands. Hannah has gone to get the truck.

Derrick lets out a squeal of excitement like a little girl that made him look very questionable. "So the plane tickets are ready?"

Alana laughs it off. "Yep. And the bags are packed."

Adam Jr. still seems nervous. "So what if they come back and ask or add something else?"

"That would be Double Jeopardy. Unless they can find something new. And they won't. You are in the clear. Just stick to the story you know and we'll all be fine."

Derrick stops to contemplate the moment. "Hmph."

Alana raises an eyebrow. "What?"

Derrick smirks. "Death by imagination huh?"

Alana smirks back with an "I got away with murder" attitude. "Yeah. Well. I guess it all depends on whose imagination you are using."

(She puts on her sunglasses and walks down the steps.)

No Honor Amongst Thieves

It is late. Alana is with Derrick at his house. Alana has poured drinks and is placing them on the table. Derrick picks it up and takes a drink. Alana is dressed in a silk negligee and straddles Derrick. They begin to kiss passionately. Derrick moans.

"Mmmmm. Nice."

"I thought so."

They kiss again.

"I am so glad that you're not my real sister."

"Yeah?"

"Yeah."

"And why is that?"

"Because I wouldn't be able to do this."

He lays her on her back and began to make love to her. He takes his glass of wine, lifts up her negligee and pours it into her belly button where he begins to drink from. Feeling powerful he downs the glass of wine in one swallow. Alana smiles in amazement. He continues to kiss her all over her body. As time progresses on, he notices that he feels strange. He grabs his head – then his heart.

He screams out in pain. "Ugh!" He tries to stand, but he falls to the floor.

Alana slides away. She speaks coolly. "What's wrong baby? (She grabs his head.) Feeling funny? Huh? Oh yeah. That's right. You see, Finley and John were on to something. (She gets up and gets dressed.) When they put that shit in me, I got to thinking. No more imagination. Just death. And that sweetheart, is what I needed."

"Why? I thought you loved me?"

"Love you? I do. But there's someone else I love even more."

"Who? What?"

She looks at him sternly and laughs. "Your brother. He's the better lover."

"Are you kidding me? After all I have done for you?"

"Mmm. Mmm. No. I'm not."

There is a light knock on door. Alana walks over and opens the door. Adam quickly steps in.

"Is it done?"

"Yeah. She's dead."

"Good."

"And your end?"

She gestures over to where Derrick is lying on the floor dying. Derrick looks up at Adam Jr. in disbelief. Adam turns his head.

"All loose ends are tied then?"

"Yep. All except for one."

"What's that?"

"You." She pulls out her gun that is now equipped with a silencer and kills Adam Jr.

She cleans up and stages the room to look like a murder suicide. She injects Adam, with dissolved pills she took from a bottle, in the foot. She places the gun in his hand. She leaves without being seen.

The next morning Alana plans her get away. Everything was set. She did not care for any inheritance as she had emptied all the accounts of her family. At this point she just wanted to disappear. She boards her plane looking at all the flights she has checked in for. Good luck finding her. She knew that everyone would be looking for her so she devised it where she will be on an airplane literally for the next week until she reaches her final destination.

Epilogue

It is one year later. Alana is on the beach. She is actually glowing and smiling. Although very single, she has met a few men who can relieve her of her desires. Today, she knew that she had something to do. Her phone rings from a number she thought she may have recognized. The odd thing is – she left or destroyed anything that could trace back to her. She decides to answer anyway.

"Hello?"

"Hello Alana." It's a woman's voice. Why does she recognize it?

"Who is this?"

"That doesn't matter. What does matter is I know what you did."

Alana looks around suspiciously. "I don't know what you're talking about."

"OK. Let's go with that. I'll put it to you this way, Derrick had plans too and I was part of it until you changed things."

"Oh Hannah. I was the only woman in his life that actually mattered."

"You think so?"

"Yeah, I *know* so."

"He *loved* me'"

"No bitch. He loved fucking you. Better yet controlling you."

"Well, I tell you what. Since you took everything from me, I'm going to take something from you. Guess you never *imagined* that."

There is a single gunshot.

"NO. My imagination is much more vivid than that."

Alana disconnects the call when a text from a hidden number comes through. All it states is: **DONE**

She smiles and places the phone back in her pocket.

A Word from the Author

Freshman year of high school is where it all began. I will never forget how ALL of my English teachers looked forward to my work (mainly my short stories)! One teacher even told me that I had a gift! I didn't realize it then, but I'm learning to embrace that realization.

It had always been my dream to be a published author. I wrote Death by Imagination (birthed in 2009) strictly to entertain. It was originally written as a script for which I had plans to develop into a movie (that could still happen), but over the course of time and after much research, I realized there was much more involved with that process, so I decided to turn it into manuscript instead. We all know that the book usually comes first anyway!

Alana Wells, the main character, is conflicted with life. Should she stay or go? Does she follow her heart or does she remain loyal to her job? Among the chaos (both personally and professionally), Alana has a decision to make. The question is ... will it be the right one for her?

I can identify with Alana. My own journey has not been easy either. Amongst the tough decisions, there were many time I wanted to give up, but now that I'm finished, I'm so glad that I didn't!

As a writer, this experience has helped me to grow and mature. I've found new confidence and gained an appreciation for the craft. Although it is not easy, it is worth it. I know that deep down inside, THIS is what I am meant to do!

I hope you enjoy!

Patricia Brothers
Author

About the Author

Patricia Brothers was born and raised in St. Louis, MO. She is a mother of two. She is currently working on her degree in Organizational Leadership with an emphasis in Psychology. In her high school days, writing and acting were a part of her favorite past times. She has been the lead actress in 2 plays and held multiple supporting roles. Being an author has always been her dream. While she has held many positions in the corporate world, she never let go of her dream.

Follow the author on Social Media:

FaceBook: Patricia Brothers (Author)

Instagram and Twitter: @TriciaBwriting

Email: TriciaBWriting@gmail.com

Questions for Thought

- ❖ How do you feel about Alana?
- ❖ Do you see anything wrong with her lustful ways?
- ❖ Did it surprise you when she killed the members of her surviving family?
- ❖ Although the brothers were adopted, does it surprise you that she was involved romantically?
- ❖ Should Detective Finley have told the Chief of their plans to leave the country?
  - ○ What would you have done?
  - ○ Does it matter since his plans were to kill them anyway?
- ❖ What was your favorite part of the book?
- ❖ Could anything have gone any other way?
- ❖ It seems the motives were greed, jealousy and hate – where did things go wrong?
- ❖ Thinking back, T.J. White was having an affair with his secretary. He called her his work wife.
  - ○ Did she deserve any of his insurance money?
  - ○ If you were the wife, would you have helped to take care of the baby?
  - ○ How do these work place affairs start?
  - ○ Is flirting cheating?
- ❖ What do you think of the Wells family as a whole?

Black Butterfly Books

an imprint of

The Butterfly Typeface Publishing.

Books to intelligently entertain the discriminating reader!

Contact us for all your

publishing & writing needs!

Iris M Williams

PO Box 56193

Little Rock AR 72215

www.butterflytypeface.com

Made in the USA
San Bernardino, CA
23 August 2017